CALL to the BLUE RIDGE

By

Raymond Houston Minter

12/01/06

To Mrs. Dominy

God Bless you.

Raymond H. Minter

DEDICATION

I wish to pay tribute to my wife, Helen,
whose insight and intellect have guided me in this work.
Her love, encouragement, constructive criticism, proofing, and
typing have been invaluable. It is to her that I dedicate this book.

* * * * *

I further wish to thank my good friend, Allie Orr,
for his encouragement to complete this work which I started twenty
years earlier.

TABLE OF CONTENTS

CHAPTER 1

Now the Lord had said unto Abram,
get thee out of thy country, and from thy kindred,
and from thy father's house,
unto a land that I will shew thee.
...and I will bless thee...
...and will make thee a blessing.
Genesis 12 KJV

And so it was that I should leave a secure position in the city to follow a compulsion I knew to be the call of God...a Call to the Blue Ridge. I came with no promise of great monetary gain or security. Nevertheless, I had an unquenchable thirst to care for God's sheep and a driving spirit to share God's love among His people. I'm Matthew Slater.

As my wife, Helen, and I drove north from Atlanta toward the mountains of North Georgia that October day, the fiery leaves of autumn were already beginning to fall and the gray skies were promising to fulfill the awaited arrival of winter. We knew it would be turning cold soon and we wanted to be settled in our new home before the snow fell. All signs and weather forecasts predicted an early winter. Thanksgiving was always special and it would be the first holiday in our new home. Our destination was a community called Stone Gap a few miles from the North Carolina line.

The car was warm but we could tell it was getting colder outside as the windows began fogging up. We could see the mist and fog engulf the higher peaks like smoke from a smoldering campfire. What was ahead for us was as much a mystery as what was around the next bend in the road. We had accepted this opportunity to move into full-time ministry on faith alone. We knew no one except Him who had called us, and in this confidence we drove on. In the back of my mind I was asking myself if it were fair to bring my wife into this situation, uncertain as it was. The answer kept coming back to me that Helen had felt the same calling as I, so it was not just I but both of us who were obeying God's voice.

I must take time to describe the magnificent beauty of these hills...the wooded mountains with evergreens mingled with hardwoods...the cultivated bottomland with corn still in brown shucks...the fall crops of turnip greens, collards, cabbage, and kale, and pastures that looked as if an artist had etched them on canvas. I knew the streams here were cold and pure and I could envision trout swimming over the rocky bottoms. These mountains are the eastern most range of the Appalachians, sharing their splendor from north Georgia to southern Pennsylvania. Yes, this is the Blue Ridge. The scenery was certainly to my liking. Since I was a small boy I have enjoyed hunting and fishing or almost anything having to do with the out-of-doors.

As we arrived at Stone Gap I realized how accurately descriptive the name was. On both sides of the road were huge boulders protruding out of the faces of opposing mountains. After a gasp and several minutes of just soaking up the beauty of this setting, reality rudely made me aware that I was looking for Stone Gap Church. In such a small community , I figured we could spot the church if we drove around for a few minutes. Yes, and I was right, for within five minutes there it was. The marquis read "Stone Gap Church"...The pastor line was blank. I chuckled to Helen, "I hope the Pastor's line being blank will not be indicative of my ministry here".

It was a lovely white frame church with a steeple. The paint was new and, from first impression, I surmised it to be well kept. The grass, though browning, was neat and the shrubs well trimmed. A further glance showed a cemetery just as well kept. I thought to myself, "these people really care".

Someone came from around the corner of the church, then another. They were both smiling. "I reckon you're the new Pastor," one of them said.

"Yes, my name is Matthew Slater and this is my wife, Helen".

"My name is Alton Jones", he said, "and this is my brother, Tommy. We were just picking up some limbs that were blown down a couple of days ago."

After getting acquainted and talking for a while, we asked directions to the parsonage.

"You folks are welcome to eat supper with us tonight," Alton said. After getting directions, we agreed to be at his home at 6 o'clock that evening.

Everything looked great outside the church but we hadn't been inside yet. As we entered through the double doors, the outside world vanished and we were engulfed in an atmosphere of warmth and love. The Jones brothers had gone and no one was visible but Helen and me, but I could feel another presence. I knew this was the same gentle spirit that had first begun to prompt us and direct us to leave our home and jobs and come to this remote setting. The simple beauty of this sanctuary was inspiring but the spirit was overwhelming. After we prayed, Helen reminded me that the parsonage awaited us and quoted the scripture "Work while it is day for when night cometh no man can work"! I'm glad she has a sense of humor. After a few more minutes we went outside and looked at the church again.

"It's a great feeling to be here", I told Helen. As we drove out of the churchyard a chilling breeze was blowing leaves across the road. I was again reminded of the necessity of getting settled in for winter. How I love this time of year.

Alton's instructions were very good and in about twenty minutes we were at the parsonage. It really wasn't that far but the last mile was not paved and the road was pretty rough.

"Well here it is", I said as we got out of the car. The whole panorama was like something out of a storybook. The house was on a small rise with foothills and then mountains in the background. Each succeeding peak gave way to the next until they blended into the distant afternoon horizon. A flowering meadow slipped out of the lesser hills toward us, interrupted only by a glimmering stream that weaved its course in and out through the grassy terrain.

"Don't you just love these trees?" I said. And what trees they were! We had six or seven large red oaks in the yard and nothing could have pleased me more.

"That looks like an orchard," Helen said, pointing to a grove of trees to our right.

"I'll look it over when I get time", I said.

My excitement was already at a peak and I hadn't even gotten to the porch. As I opened the door, Helen paused and I immediately picked up on her thoughts. We had been married for ten years but she still wanted me to carry her across the threshold. Once that was accomplished, a kiss followed and we began exploring the house. It was a modest cottage with a living room, dining room, kitchen, two bedrooms, a den, and a small study. Nothing was oversized but adequate.

"Only one bath", I said. She smiled knowing I was thinking of all the times I was trying to put on my tie while competing with her for the mirror.

"Well, maybe we can add another one in time", she said. The kitchen and dining room were across the back of the house with windows facing the mountains. The dining room had a bay window so one could enjoy the view while eating. Helen was very pleased and I knew this would also be her favorite spot for studying the bible or sewing or whatever reason she could come up with to use this area. I knew lots of my time would be spent in the study praying and preparing sermons. No cottage such as this would be complete without a fireplace and sure enough, our den had one. It was arched and had a very old mantle that looked like it had been made from heart pine. I thought to myself "whoever designed this house was my kind of guy". By the time we had looked everything over, it was 5:15 and, in the excitement, we had forgotten that we had no place to stay for the night. Our furniture was not to arrive until the next day.

"I'm glad today is Tuesday", I said. I knew it would take the rest of the week to arrange and rearrange furniture. A pastor's wife is no different from any other in that respect and yes, I'm another "honey-do" husband - "Honey do this"…"Honey do that." I couldn't help but grin a little thinking about it.

"We had better go", I told Helen. "We don't want to be late".

Alton's directions took us back through Stone Gap and into a setting of rolling hills of spruce, hickory, and oak with patches of pasture here and there. Houses were sparsely scattered but close enough if you had need of a neighbor. Several homes had chicken houses nearby. This was not foreign to me. I knew that many north Georgia farmers supplemented their income by raising chickens. Already the sun was beginning to slide behind the hills and I could see smoke rising from many chimneys.

"It gets cool pretty fast up here when the sun goes down," I said, remembering some of my camping experiences in the mountains.

The mailbox read *A. Jones*, and I recognized Al's Chevy truck. As we pulled into the driveway, the front door opened and out ran three children, the oldest I guessed to be about twelve years old.

"Mom, the new preacher's here". The children were all around us as we got out of the car.

"Well, where did all these girls come from?" I asked teasingly, knowing full well the oldest was a boy. He just grinned. Alton and his wife were coming down the walk by this time.

"Honey, this is Pastor Slater and his wife, Helen," Alton said. "This is my wife, Sue, and these are three of our children- Nathan, Betsy, and Tom".

Alton and Sue didn't look all that well matched. He was tall, well muscled, with sandy hair and blue eyes. Sue was petite and pretty, with brown hair and brown eyes. I noted that the children inherited their father's hair and eyes although each seemed to favor Sue. Well, I guess they were pretty well matched after all.

"We have another daughter inside", Sue said. "Come in and meet her". As we entered the house we were greeted by the smell of food and the warm glow of a fireplace.

"Robin", Sue called, " we have company". In a hustle, a little girl in a wheelchair rushed into the room.

"This is our daughter, Robin. She's eight".

Another beautiful child she was too, with the same sandy hair and blue eyes as the other three. She was brimming with energy and her countenance radiated with excitement. As the ladies walked into the kitchen, Al and I sat on the sofa facing the fireplace.

"You've got a fine family", I said. I wanted to know about Robin's condition but didn't ask at this time.

"Weather's turning cold", Al said.

"Yes, it is", I agreed. "Do you get much snow up here in winter?"

"Yes, we do", he said. It usually snows some in late November and in December but the heaviest snowfall is in January and February".

"I have always liked snow", I said. "I never saw much though until I was in the Army in Germany."

"Were you in Germany, too?" Al asked. As we talked, I found that we had served there about five years apart. Having covered two of the most talked about subjects among newly acquainted men, the weather and military service, I was about to ask about Robin when Sue called us to supper.

The table was filled with a variety of good things to eat and I knew we had a treat in store. With every child in his place at the table, Alton asked me to pray. I must confess, I probably cut it a little short... I was starved! Everything was so good, nothing really fancy, but plentiful.

"Sue, this is a fine meal", I said.

"Yes, it's delicious", Helen added.

We talked about the church, community, and local things in general but all the while we were talking, I kept noticing an extra place at the table. I guess my curiosity was obvious when Sue said the other place setting was for Tommy, Alton's brother, whom we had met at the church that afternoon. I learned that Tommy was single and lived with them.

"He seems to be a nice person", I said. "Do you have other family?" I asked.

"Yes, we have one sister, Mary Katherine, who attends North Georgia College in Dahlonega. She's four years younger than Tommy", Alton replied. "They are having a winter retreat during Thanksgiving so she will not be home until Christmas break".

When we were about halfway through the meal, the door opened and I heard Tommy's voice.

"I'm home. Sorry I'm late but two cows got out and I had to round them up and get them back inside the fence."

A young man I judged to be about twenty-four or twenty-five, Tommy was tall like Alton and ruggedly handsome. He had brown hair and gentle, yet searching, blue eyes. I hadn't noticed with our brief encounter earlier but he walked with a slight limp.

"Rev. Slater and I were just talking about our Army days", Alton said. "Tommy is the hero around here".

Tommy blushed and said he had been drafted and served in Vietnam. It was obvious that he didn't want to talk about it so I didn't ask any questions.

After a delicious meal, the ladies sent us men off to the den with a promise of pie and coffee later. I was glad for this time alone with the men so we could get better acquainted. I had a good feeling about this family and wanted to get to know them. I was particularly drawn to two of them, little Robin and Tommy. As we sat watching the flames flickering in the fireplace, Alton again mentioned Tommy' s military service.

"Tommy received the Medal of Honor in Vietnam", Alton said.

With this, I asked Tommy to tell me about it. He was a little reluctant at first but after a few sentences, he seemed to open up. He had been drafted and was in Vietnam within five months. His infantry unit was penned down in a crossfire. The enemy had every advantage. Tommy saw many of his buddies killed and many more wounded and dying. With his squad leader dead, Tommy crawled seventy-five yards through open terrain. He then charged the enemy position on his right knocking out their machine gun and opening up a route of escape for his squad. I saw Tommy hesitate several times while relating the events of that day. A couple of times I saw tears come to his eyes and I felt he was holding in lots of pain. I made myself a promise that one day we would talk again on this matter. Tommy had been wounded twice that day in the lower leg and in his foot. Because of his heroic action he had received the Medal of Honor. Not through any disinterest on my part, I changed the subject to church matters.

"How many members attend our church?" I asked.

"About fifty or fifty-five I'd say", Alton replied, and about that many more who attend regularly but who are not members."

I realize that isn't a large congregation by any standard. However, to be my first church, the responsibility weighed heavily upon me. Oh, I had spoken on many occasions in church, in nursing homes, etc. Those were temporary responsibilities. Being a pastor requires full-time commitment.

"How many churches are here?" I questioned.

"Just ours", Alton said.

"About how many people live in Stone Gap and the surrounding area?" I asked.

"Around four hundred, wouldn't you say, Tommy?"

"Yes, around four hundred", Tommy replied.

After pie and coffee we talked a while longer. Noticing the clock, I realized the evening had gotten away. We were about to say goodnight when Sue asked us where we were spending the night. I told her we would be staying in a motel.

"Will you stay with us? We have plenty of room and would be pleased if you would stay".

Feeling very much at home, we accepted the invitation. We were pleased not having to drive twenty miles to a motel. After getting our luggage from the car we said goodnight and were off to bed.

I had learned a few things about our new environment but was glad to be alone with Helen to find out what she had learned. As we lay in bed that first night at Stone Gap, I can't explain the peaceful feeling I had thinking about our new life. I found that Helen was as excited as I. We talked low for a while and then, as the house grew quiet, we whispered. As we exchanged bits of information, I learned that Robin had fallen on an icy step and had injured her spine. Sue told Helen that numerous tests had been made and the ultimate conclusion was that Robin would probably never walk again. I was deeply touched as she told me this. Robin was so much alive! Quite some time elapsed before our whispers gave way to peaceful slumber. It seemed like only moments when we were awakened and, much to my surprise, it was morning and I felt fully rested.

"Boy! A man could grow old fast around here if all the time goes by as fast as the night did", I said.

Helen smiled in agreement. It was already 7:30 and I could smell breakfast cooking. As we made our way to the dining room, I knew I needed a good meal in order to face the day moving furniture.

The drive back to the parsonage was very pleasant. The day was clear and the chill in the air was slowly giving way to the warming rays of morning sun. When we arrived "home" we had only a short wait before our furniture arrived.

"I'm surprised that you found us so quickly", I told the driver.

"Well, Rev. Slater, we just found the church and got instructions from there", the driver said.

Fortunately for us, the house was ready to move into except for a little dusting. Room by room, it started filling up and began looking like home with the addition of each familiar piece of furniture. Having completely unloaded the truck, the moving crew was off, leaving Helen and me along.

"Oh, it's going to be a lovely home", Helen, said.

Each day that followed brought a little more order to our cottage and by Friday evening almost everything was in place.

I had been thinking all week about Sunday morning. The day after tomorrow would be my first sermon. I quietly slipped away from the interior decorator role and sought the privacy of my study. I opened my Bible and read where I had underlined St. John 9:4. "*I must work the works of Him that sent me while it is day; the night cometh when no man can work.*"

Ironically, that was the same scripture Helen had quoted only a few days earlier. What better verse could have summed up my feelings? This was, I felt, an answer to my prayers and a sign that my Father was aware of my desire to do His will. As I dried my eyes, the room seemed to be charged with the presence of God. My first sermon would be entitled "My Father's Son".

CHAPTER 2

I t was a beautiful Sunday morning and we were up early.
"I don't think I've been this excited since our wedding", I said.
"I feel the same way", Helen replied.

We hurried so we could be at church before anyone else arrived.
And so we were. I immediately noticed the marquis, <u>Stone Gap
Church - Rev. Matthew Slater, Pastor</u>. I was pleased.

After a short while people started arriving and Helen and I
greeted each one as he came into the church. Alton had said about a
hundred people attended regularly. To the best of my ability I
counted 137, and I knew I had probably missed some of the smaller
children. As the congregation sang, all eyes were on me; as the
offering plate was passed, all eyes were on me; as the choir sang, all
eyes were on me.

After a formal introduction by a deacon, I was alone behind the
pulpit. I made a few introductory remarks about Helen and me.
Then, after having prayer, I opened my Bible and began.

"<u>I am my Father's Son</u>. My text is St. John 9:4; *I must work the
works of Him that sent me while it is day; the night cometh when no
man can work.* My father was a carpenter. His work as a builder of
houses started with the most basic but important undertaking, that
of providing a strong foundation. He endeavored to instill in my
young mind the importance of beginning a building well and building thereon with confidence. This same principle applied to my
spiritual upbringing as well. When I was a child, my father was the

highest authority in our home. In all areas of family life, my father guided us. If we had a question, we asked him. He was there to help us and, yes, sometimes to discipline us. He always provided for our needs and most of the time, he provided our desires as well. You see my father had our best interest in mind. He truly loved us."

I continued; "Through this loving relationship, I grew to adore my Father and willingly obeyed and respected him. And so it is with our Heavenly Father. He is always there to guide us. When we have questions, we can ask Him for the answers. He's always there to help us and yes, sometimes to correct us. He always provides for our needs and most of the time, He gives us our desires. You see our Heavenly Father has our best interest in mind. He has provided a way for us to have an intimate relationship with Him through His son, Jesus. This avenue to the Father is open to everyone who will accept it. Will you accept His offer to you as I have? God truly loves us. I adore my Heavenly Father and willingly obey Him. I answer His voice and seek to do His will. It is through this loving relationship that I have come to be your Pastor." After the invitation and prayer, I concluded by saying, "God truly loves us."

Sometimes it's hard to judge how well people receive a message but I knew that I had delivered to them what I had received from God. I hoped it had touched them as much as it had me.

As the congregation stood for dismissal, I saw Helen beaming and wiping her eyes. I knew she was with me all the way. Immediately after the "Amen", I made my way to her. She gripped my hand as people thronged around us. It felt great!

How would I ever get all the names straight and remember whose baby was whose. Even with the crowd around, I became aware of something tugging at my coat. I turned and looked down. There was Robin in her wheelchair. She was holding her Bible on her lap. Her sandy hair flowed smoothly over her blue dress, blue the color of her eyes.

"How are you this morning? I'm very glad to see you", I said.

"Just fine," she replied energetically. "When are you coming back to my house?" I told her we would come again soon. The congregation was gracious and warm and we had many invitations for Sunday dinner. With each, however, we took "rain checks". This was our first Sunday afternoon in our new home and we wanted it to be ours alone. Besides, to be quite honest, I was exhausted and welcomed the opportunity to relax after such a demanding week.

The bright Sunday afternoon soon gave way to the shadows of early evening as the sun began to slip behind the hills. By the time the evening service started at 6 o'clock, it was dark. The congregation was large, much to my pleasure. So many beautiful people! My joy again overwhelmed me as the congregation was singing. Everyone seemed to unite in one spirit as they sang "Holy, Holy".

There were several people who caught my attention, but one couple really stood out to me. An older couple on the second row near the aisle was singing with great enthusiasm. As "Holy Holy" gave way to "Amazing Grace", tears were rolling down their faces. The man kept wiping his eyes. It seemed he would dry his cheeks just before the tears reached his beard. He had such a lovely silver gray beard . His wife was radiant. Her bespectacled eyes were aglow with life.

"We must get acquainted with them", I thought.

After my message and the invitation we adjourned and Helen and I made our way to where the old couple was.

"How are you folks tonight?" I asked. They told us their names were Aaron and Daisy McHenry. As we talked briefly, for many people were coming by to greet us, I felt a real kinship with them. They were both very gracious and welcomed us to visit their home. We said goodnight to them and were again engulfed in the crowd.

"What a fulfilling evening", I sighed as we drove home that night.

Helen agreed and added, "Weren't the McHenrys lovely people?"

"They certainly were. I want to visit them this week."

I realized that to do justice to my church I must very methodically search out and visit each family. The church secretary, Mrs. Chastain, had given me a list of members and their addresses.

"Honey, if I really work hard at it, I believe I can visit every family by Thanksgiving".

The first thing Monday morning, the McHenrys came to mind so I told Helen, "There's no time like the present to visit them." She agreed and said she would be ready to go with me just as soon as she could put away the breakfast dishes.

As it turned out, Aaron and Daisy lived only three miles from us. They had a rustic log house very neatly maintained. Behind their house was a log barn. Except for power lines, one could have mistaken this setting for a scene from the late 1800's.

Daisy was raking leaves when we arrived but immediately propped her rake against a tree. She welcomed us and said Aaron was out back taking care of the animals. I told her I would find him. As the ladies chatted, I walked toward the barn. Approaching the barnyard, I was welcomed by several goats, chickens, ducks, and calves. I peeked inside the barn and saw Aaron milking a goat. He didn't look up at first and I hesitated to speak for a moment for fear I might startle him.

"Come on in Reverend", he said.

"How did you know I was here?" I asked.

He said he had noticed the animals moving toward the barnyard gate and heard the hens clucking excitedly. "I knew someone was here when the animals told me."

I nodded in understanding.

"You ever milked a goat?" he asked.

"No, only cows", I said.

"You want to"?

"Sure, why not!" Without hesitation I straddled the milking stool and adjusted the bucket so I could hit it.

"OK, goat", I said. "If you will cooperate with me, I'll cooperate with you". I guess my hands were a bit cold because the goat flinched a little when I first started. Aaron laughed and seemed surprised that I obliged him so readily.

"Has this goat got a name, Brother McHenry?" I asked.

"Yes, Sir, she has", he replied. "Just call her Jenny and call me Pa Mac".

"That's just fine," I said. "My name is Matthew. Mac and Matthew...We sound like twins!"

He laughed so hard that he almost knocked over the milk bucket. I thanked Jenny for standing still and she just looked around at me as if she understood what I had said.

As Aaron showed me around the barnyard, I asked him how much livestock he had.

"Well, I've got five goats with more on the way, three calves, fifteen chickens, seven ducks, and a mule named Ole Jack". Ole Jack", he explained, "likes to graze down by the branch. I don't work him much any more. I just like to keep him around the place to go huntin' with me. I gotta tell you a story bout Ole Jack...Why, he's the best pointer in these hills... quail, that is. Ole Jack, points quail. Why, one day a neighbor and I were out huntin'. Ole Jack had pointed three coveys of birds"...

Aaron's gray eyes were twinkling as he continued. "Then he near 'bout embarrassed me to death! As we topped this hill, Old Jack broke and ran down toward the creek. My neighbor was real disappointed and asked what he was doing. I said I was sorry 'bout the way Ole Jack was behavin but the only thing he likes to do better than pointin' birds is fishin!"

By this time, this preacher, Matthew Slater, knew he had his hands full keeping up with Pa Mac. As we laughed and talked, Aaron picked up the milk bucket and walked toward the house.

"It's so refreshing to be outside on days like today", I said. Aaron said he had farmed most of his life and had a feel for the land. I knew what he meant. How can you explain to someone the feeling you get when you smell the freshly plowed earth and see the furrowed fields ready to be planted?

Daisy and Helen were looking at flowers in the yard as we approached the house. Daisy invited us in and offered us coffee.

"That sounds just fine to me", I said.

"Would yall like some sweet potato pie?"

"We'd love some sweet potato pie", Helen replied.

We listened more than we talked as we fellowshipped with this special couple. Aaron said he had been born in that same house seventy years ago. He and Daisy had been married for forty-seven years. They had two sons born to them. One had died as an infant and the other was killed in the Korean War. Not having any living offspring, they said that they had unofficially adopted nearly every young person in Stone Gap to be their child or grandchild. "That's why we are called Pa and Ma Mac", Daisy said.

Their account of personal tragedy and grief made me to realize all the more the "peace of God which passeth all understanding". Only the peace of God could have brought them through all this and still allow them to be as pleasant and noticeably content as they were. My, how interesting they were to listen to and how warm they were toward us.

Daisy told us that Aaron's grandfather had built their house in 1885. I marveled at how well built and how well preserved it was. "Everything is almost the same now as when Grandpa McHenry built it except for the electric lights and plumbing", she said.

Daisy showed us her wedding ring. It was a very old, very ornate gold ring that had belonged to Aaron's Grandmother. "I am as proud of it now as I was the first time I saw it," she beamed.

A quick glance at my watch told me the morning had gotten away. We stood up to leave when Aaron asked me if I liked peanuts. I assured him I did. Without hesitation he went into a back room, a pantry I suppose, and came back in a few minutes with about a peck of peanuts. Then Daisy asked us to wait a minute longer as she went into the pantry. When she returned she had two quart jars of green beans and two pints of pickles. "Folks around here don't have lots of money but we like to make sure our Pastor doesn't go hungry", she said.

"How sweet of you! Thank you so much", Helen told her.

Before leaving, we had prayer and were hugged by them. On the way home I told Helen, "I'll never forget today. I wish all old folks could be as gracious as Pa and Ma Mac."

That afternoon I drove into Stone Gap to get my car serviced and to meet some more of the community. Harry Chance operated the gas station and general store. I introduced myself and told him I needed a lube and oil change. Harry was nice enough but didn't say much. Waiting for him to finish with my car, I kept trying to remember if he were at church on Sunday. Rather than embarrass him or myself I avoided asking him. Today I would just be cordial. Moving slowly sometimes is best. When Harry finished, I paid him and asked if there were a barbershop in the village. He pointed me in the right direction and told me to look for Ned's Barbershop.

There it was, NED J. BENSON, BARBER. I wasn't in dire

need of a haircut but I wanted to feel the pulse of the community. There's no better place to do that than at the barbershop. *Ting-a-ling*, went the bell as I entered. Ned Benson was a big man, very tall and, ironically, very bald. I took a seat to wait for my turn in the chair. There was one man in the chair and one man ahead of me. Three other men were just sitting around a wood stove talking. Not knowing or being known of anyone, I just picked up a newspaper and began to glance over it as the normal conversations resumed.

"They're predicating more snow this year than normal", one man said.

"Yeah, gonna be a cold winter I hear".

"Must be so cause the wooly worm has a thicker than normal coat and the corn shucks were thicker this year."

"Anybody shot a deer yet?"

"Shot one but he got away." They had just hit on one of my favorite pastimes.

"Is the hunting good around here?" I asked.

"Pretty good" one man volunteered. I knew that I was now in the conversation so I introduced myself. Upon learning that I was a minister, the conversations continued but the men were a little less generous with expletives.

"Do the deer grow very large?" I asked.

"Yes sir, Reverend", another man said. "A few years ago Tommy Jones killed a nice 14 pointer."

"Yeah, he's one of the best hunters in these parts", Ned added. "Funny thing about Tommy though. He hasn't even picked up a gun since he got home from the Army."

"Next!"

My train of thought was broken as Ned called for the next customer. The conversation went to something else as if someone had thrown a switch. "Did you hear who got locked up Saturday night over in Blue Ridge"?

"No, who?"

"The Anderson boys."

"I'm not surprised. They're both hell raisers. Excuse me Reverend. Those two boys are wild as bucks. Raised in a Christian home, too", Ned said.

"Next!"

I climbed into the chair and became the focal point as conversation died down. I felt as if I had been given the podium to deliver a sermon. "A little off the top please and not too high on the sides", I told Ned.

Conversation resumed as Ned flipped on his clippers. I noticed a tattoo on his right arm. "Were you in the Navy?" I asked.

"Yes, sir", three years and eleven months."

"I was in the army myself", I told him. "By the way, Ned, how about taking some of the hair you're cutting off the sides and put it on top where it's so thin." A roar went up from everyone.

"If I could do that, I'd be a rich man", Ned replied. "Besides, you don't have enough hair on the sides to cover the top!" Well, one good laugh deserves another, I thought.

"I'll tell you how to save your hair though, Reverend, if you like".

"How's that?" I replied.

"I'll give you a cigar box to save it in". Another roar went up.

"Thanks. I'll have to remember that", I said smiling.

"Were you born here in Stone Gap, Ned?" I asked.

"No Reverend. I came here about twenty years ago."

"Where are you from?" I asked.

"Well, I grew up in Vinings which was only a village then. It's between Marietta and Atlanta. I think they sell property there now by the inch."

"I know the area well. Do you have relatives still there?"

"Oh, no. I never knew my dad. He was killed in the war. My Mom passed away when I was only six days old. I was raised in an orphanage and came here right out of the military. I married a girl from Stone Gap."

"Your sign says NED J BENSON. What does the J stand for?" I asked.

He laughed and said it stands for Johnston. I was named after Confederate General Joseph E. Johnston who commanded the Confederacy in Georgia against General Sherman. My Mom made Johnston my middle name because it was my father's middle name. I don't know where she came up with Ned."

As Ned finished, I asked him how much.

"This one is on me, Reverend."

I thanked him and told everyone how good it was to meet each of them. As the door closed behind me, the ringing of the bell made me realize that the afternoon was well spent. All of God's work isn't done in church.

On the way home I was praying for God's will to be done through Helen and me. I knew God's direction was crucial to our success in Stone Gap. I knew, too, that God had everything under control and all was well if we would only seek His guidance.

As I reached our home, Helen met me at the door. "Honey, the Farleys have a sick child and want you to come and pray for him."

"Oh", I said, "Do you want to go with me?"

"I do, but I'm in the middle of preparing dinner", she said. With a quick kiss, I was off to the Farley's house.

With the advent of health insurance, I feel that many have forsaken the age-old reliance on God's healing and sustaining power. We have chosen the tangible for the intangible. Many in Stone Gap still followed the "old ways".

The Farleys lived about five miles away but with all the bumps and curves, I guess it must have taken fifteen minutes to get there. I was praying for the child and for the family in general, even though I was still a little foggy as to who the Farleys were. I had met so many people but had gotten to really know only a few of them so far. As I drove up, I immediately recognized Jeff Farley as someone I had met but only briefly talked with at church. Jeff and Shirley Farley were a couple in their mid-twenties. They had one son and one daughter.

"Our son is sick", Jeff said. "He has a very high fever".

"Well, Jeff", I said, "I believe in the power of prayer".

As Jeff, Shirley, and I stood by the sick child's bed, I opened my bible and read from James 5:14-15a. I had them follow the reading in their bible. "...*Is any sick among you? Let him call for the elders of the church; and let them pray over him, anointing him with oil in the name of the Lord: And the prayer of faith shall save the sick, and the Lord shall raise him up.*"

"Now, Jeff and Shirley", I said, "We have read the scriptures concerning prayer and healing. Although we believe in divine healing and have a measure of faith in us as Christians, still it is good to review and to read for ourselves what the word says. Now let us anoint your child with oil and pray." As I took the small bottle of oil from my coat pocket and gently anointed the child's head, I felt the fever on his brow. As we prayed, I sensed that he had been touched by the Lord.

I stayed a while and talked with Jeff and Shirley. They were very fine people, very much in love. I felt really good about being their pastor. Just before I left, we looked in on the boy again and found him sitting up in bed playing with a matchbox car. I wasn't surprised to see that his fever had gone down; however, I am always amazed at the way Jesus works. As I left, they thanked me for coming.

"We'll see you Sunday", Jeff said. God had proven Himself again to me. Now, as it was already beginning to get dark, I looked forward to getting home and eating supper.

CHAPTER 3

Time slipped by so fast that first month. Our days were filled with visitation and caring for the needs of our people. We always wanted to be available when we were needed. The cool days became shorter and grayer as the holiday season approached. We really looked forward to this Thanksgiving. This year it seemed to have taken on a very special meaning to us. We had so much for which to be thankful.

The congregation planned to have a Thanksgiving meal at church where everyone could eat together. That sounded like a good idea to me. After having been there a little over a month, Helen and I had eaten many meals with many families and had experienced some great cooking.

Following the Sunday evening service, Alton Jones asked me if I wanted to go along on a deer hunt. I immediately checked my calendar to see if I had any appointments. "Yes, Al, I'd love to go with you", I eagerly replied. He asked me to meet him at his house at 5 o'clock on Monday morning. He told me that two or three more guys would be going with us. I had a good 30.06 rifle and a box of 150-grain bullets. I've always loved hunting and the first opportunity to hunt this year had me as excited as a child at Christmas. My excitement was not only that of hunting but also the gratification of being with these men of our church.

My alarm clock was unmerciful as it stirred me that morning at 4 o'clock. Once awake, however, and aware that this was the day, all drowsiness left. I quickly shaved and dressed, drank a cup of coffee, and ate a sweet roll. I kissed Helen goodbye, got my hunting gear, and went to the car. To my surprise, there were snow flurries. I had dressed for the cold but I didn't expect snow. I arrived at Alton's home ten minutes early and went in to have another cup of coffee.

"Pastor, today should be a good day to hunt", Al said. "The other guys will be along shortly."

As I finished my coffee, Aaron McHenry and Caleb Fisher drove up. Caleb was a member of our local congregation and a carpenter by trade. He was about forty to forty-five and very thin. He showed signs of hard work as his calluses verified when we shook hands.

"Well, Pastor, everyone is here. Are you ready to go?" Al asked.

"Come on, everybody can go together in my car", Aaron said. He was driving an antique station wagon but, in spite of its age, it performed well.

"Aaron, why didn't you bring Ole Jack along?" I asked. "Doesn't he like to deer hunt?" From the way everyone laughed, it was obvious they had heard about Ole Jack before.

After about fifteen minutes we arrived somewhere; I knew not where. We got out and walked through the woods another fifteen minutes by flashlight. Alton left a man about every hundred yards. Aaron was first, then Caleb, then me, and finally Alton turned his light out about a hundred yards past me. I had often been on a deer stand before dawn, but most of the time I knew the terrain. I knew daylight would be coming soon and I could tell more about my surroundings. The snow flurries seemed to vanish as daylight approached. First there was only a faint glow in the east, and very slowly, the first rays of light illuminated the treetops. I became aware of the birds as they began chirping and moving about. I could hear someone's rooster crowing in the far distance. The woods are very quiet this time of morning making one conscious of the most minute sounds. The sounds are there if we only take time to listen, I thought. "Father, let me hear the smallest cry of the least person in my congregation and let me be a minister to that need", I prayed.

About fifteen more minutes passed before I could see my imme-diate surroundings. Gradually the ever-increasing light pushed the darkness of the forest into nothingness and eventually, I could see clearly enough to get a shot if any game were spotted. I was sitting just below the crest of a small ridge of sparsely scattered hardwoods. My position afforded a view about seventy-five yards downhill and about that far to my left and right. An excellent position, I thought. The wind started stirring just a little and I noticed it was blowing uphill toward me. Another plus, I thought. Now, if a deer comes into range, I won't have to worry about it picking up my scent. Noticing things like light, shadows, and wind direction is very important to a successful hunt. It was something I had learned in the Army and on numerous hunting trips.

A flick of movement down the hill and to my right caught my attention. It was in range but I couldn't see what it was. There again, it moved with quick, almost jerky movements into the shadow of a big oak. A lump came into my throat and my heart started pounding. It was too small to be a deer and I had heard no sounds. *BOOM!* The solitude was shattered. The shot startled me so much I momentarily forgot what I was watching which, by the way, was a gray squirrel. Alton had fired the shot. Perhaps there would be some venison at the church on Thanksgiving after all.

Regaining my composure and breathing easier now, I again turned my attention downhill. Since Alton had picked this area to hunt, I figured he had experienced some measure of success here before. *Gobble, Gobble, Gobble* came a faint sound to my ears. There came that lump in my throat and that heavy breathing again. Then I heard it again!! That was unmistakably the sound of a wild turkey. I knew it was there and I knew I had a perfect vantage point if only it were turkey season and I had a shotgun. I could only wait. I also had learned that patience was a necessity for a successful hunt.

The wind began to pick up gradually with a flurry here and there. I knew that our chances of seeing game were decreasing in proportion to the increase of the wind. I glanced at my watch. It was 9:35 already, and we agreed to start toward the car at 10:00. I couldn't hear those turkey sounds anymore, but I knew they were real and I wanted to come back again to hunt this area. I tried to make mental notes by which to remember the spot. Before long I saw Alton dragging his deer in my direction, a big eight pointer.

As he drew closer, I whispered, "Congratulations". He smiled and we began swapping stories, whispering all the way so as not to disturb the area too much. As we walked back to the car, each man shared his experiences. Caleb had also heard turkeys and Aaron had seen the white flag of a deer as it retreated into a thicket.

"I think deer can sense danger", Aaron said.

"Not so wild a theory," I replied. "I've known many people who have said the same thing."

The ride back to Alton's home was bumpy but pleasant. The warmth and fellowship of my companions almost entirely erased the chill in the air. Upon our arrival back at Alton's house, Sue met us and invited us in for some hot chocolate. Everyone welcomed this reception with appreciation.

After standing around the fireplace a while, Aaron said, "We'll see yall Wednesday at prayer meeting," as he and Caleb left.

"I really enjoyed the hunt this morning, Al", I said. "I'd love to scout and hunt that area again. Who owns that property?"

"Tommy does", Al said.

"Did I hear my name?" came a voice from the hall as Tommy entered the room.

"I was just telling Pastor Slater that you own the land where we hunted this morning".

"It's a great place to hunt", I said.

We told Tommy about our hunt and I told him I'd love to hunt there again. He said he was free for the afternoon and asked if I wanted to go back. Somewhat surprised, yet happy about the opportunity, I said yes. I called Helen to check on her and to see if there were any messages for me. You never know when a minister may be needed. Nevertheless, there were no messages so the afternoon was free.

Tommy attended church regularly but seemed removed somehow. We had talked several times but he had never really opened up. I thought I understood his reluctance and I welcomed the chance to be alone with him this afternoon. Sue made a delicious lunch, and having eaten well, Alton, Tommy, and I walked around the farm about an hour.

Tommy suggested that we start for the woods a little early in order to do some scouting. I put my gun in his truck and he and I were on our way. I thought it strange to be going hunting with only me carrying a gun. Then I remembered what the guys had said in the barbershop about Tommy being the best hunter in these parts but not picking up a gun since coming home from Vietnam. I sensed there was more to this trip than just hunting.

As the pickup lumbered along the bumpy road to the hunting area, Tommy and I talked very freely. He would smile as he talked but his eyes cried out with sadness and pain. I knew we were only making conversation and neither of us was saying what was really on his mind. As we reached the hunting area, Tommy said we only had about three hours of daylight left. We walked into the woods, which were very still by now. No wind was blowing and the only movement I could see was a few snow flurries, which had consistently fallen throughout the afternoon. As we walked on, we came to a small brook with crystal clear water. *"...He that drinks of this water shall never thirst again,"* came the scripture to me.

"Tommy, let's get a drink of water." We both drank freely. The water was very cold and refreshing. "There is nothing like a good drink of water when you are really thirsty", I said. I had my gun in my hand but I was clearly "fishing".

"Yes, sir, you're right, Pastor Slater", Tommy said.

"That's the way it is with salvation," I continued. "Jesus has all the spiritual water we need, enough to satisfy the thirstiest person." He nodded his head in understanding. I knew there was a need but I didn't want to crowd him so I didn't pursue the subject.

As we walked on, we scouted two or three areas. I guess we had walked half an hour when we came to a good spot and sat down to wait. I couldn't really tell you where we had been that half hour. As well as I enjoy hunting, something greater had held my attention. As we sat saying nothing, as is the rule when still-hunting, I kept glancing at Tommy who was wiping his eyes. At first I thought the chill of the autumn evening was making his eyes water, but as time went on, I realized it wasn't the chill at all. I knew Tommy would have to open up by himself. Any intrusion now on my part would probably drive him inwardly again.

Gobble, Gobble, Gobble, plainly came a sound to me. Tommy

didn't even look up, nor did I. That turkey could have walked across the log I was sitting on and I don't think I would have moved.

"I'm very thirsty, Pastor Slater", Tommy said in a choked tone. "I'm very thirsty".

With those few words he began to cry openly, almost uncontrollably. He tried several times to talk but couldn't for about ten minutes. Slowly, he began talking. "Can God forgive killing other men"? He asked. "I've been home from Vietnam two years and haven't had a day's peace of mind since I got back. I grew up in a Christian home. Mom and Dad always attended church with us children. I accepted Christ when I was ten years old. When Mom and Dad passed away, I started living with Al and Sue. We were at church every time the doors were opened. When I became eighteen and graduated from high school", he continued, "the Vietnam War began really building up. I was classified 1-A by my draft board and I knew it wouldn't be long until I was called up. I was out of school the last of May, drafted in early September, and in Vietnam by late January."

He paused for a moment, swallowed and then he continued. "As I told you the first night you were at our house, I was in combat several times. The day I was wounded, I killed seventeen men. I was given a medal. I didn't want a medal for killing all those men." His voice broke as he asked, "Can God forgive me for killing?"

"Tommy, they gave you a medal, not for killing, but for bravery and for saving your own men." I related to him how David in the Bible had to kill, not only the giant, but also many other enemies of his nation. *Thou shalt not kill* means thou shalt do no murder. Fighting in a war is not murder. Premeditated killing by choice is murder. Fighting in war when called upon by your country is an obligation. Your actions," I continued, "were not a matter of choice. You had no choice about Vietnam just like I had no choice about Germany. Paul, the apostle, says in Philippians 3, for us not to look back but to *press forward forgetting those things which are behind, and reaching forth unto those things which are before, I press toward the mark for the prize of the high calling of God in Christ Jesus.* Paul, himself, had helped to murder many, many innocent Christians before his conversion." Tommy's eyes began to brighten.

"Tommy, let's pray". It was a beautiful prayer as Tommy opened up his heart to Jesus. I felt the presence of the Holy Spirit very strongly. Several minutes passed as Tommy's prayer of repentance became a prayer of joyful praise, and I knew that God's Holy Spirit had done its work. When we stopped praying, it was almost dark, but even in the dim evening light I could see a gleam in Tommy's eyes.

"This is a new day for you, Tommy", I said. Truly this was a sunrise at sunset.

Tommy's enthusiasm was wonderful to watch as we stumbled out of the dark woods that evening. Neither of us had brought a flashlight. Tommy seemed totally relieved and happy. He talked openly with laughter in his voice. His gate had picked up somewhat as if he had laid down a heavy burden. Smiling to myself, I realized that was exactly what he had done. I rejoiced all the way home that evening and could hardly wait to tell Helen the good news about Tommy.

CHAPTER 4

The next morning at breakfast as we were talking about Tommy, Helen remembered, "Oh, yes, Honey, Mrs. Chastain called to give you the phone number of that new family, you know, the Masons. Their telephone was just connected." The Masons had been in church on Sunday.

"We need to visit them soon", I replied.

The Masons, John and Sarah, were in their mid-forties. John had been transferred here to manage a sawmill. His broad shoulders and stocky build made him look like a lumberjack. His rugged exterior was deceptive though, as I discovered through conversation the next afternoon. He talked of the love of God and of grace and mercy and peace. It was evident that John had a relationship with Jesus. "Praise God", I thought. Sarah took Helen into the kitchen as she prepared coffee. She had spoken very little but nodded in agreement as John told of God's goodness to them.

I had noticed pictures as I entered their home.

"Do you have children?" I asked.

"Yes, we have one daughter," Sarah said. "Her name is Paula. She is in her last year of nursing school and will be home for Thanksgiving".

"That's great", I said. "There is a real need here for medical care. The nearest hospital is in Blue Ridge."

"We're having Thanksgiving dinner at church," Helen said. "I hope you and John can come and bring Paula with you".

"I'm sure we would all enjoy that", Sarah replied.

A couple of days later my phone rang about 8:30 in the morning. It was Tommy. He gasped as if he had been running. "Pastor Slater, there's been an accident. That new man at church, Mr. Mason, has been hurt."

I got directions to where John was and told Tommy to wait there for me. John, who had been with some loggers, was entering a stand of timber that was being cut. The logger who was cutting the trees didn't hear John's jeep approaching because of the noise of the chain saw. The tree he was cutting fell across John's jeep. The details were sketchy. The tract of timber being cut was near Tommy's home. He had found out about the accident and called me at once.

I didn't know what to expect when I arrived. It was only a few miles but what a long time to get there, it seemed. As I rounded the curve in the road, I saw Tommy waving to me. I jumped from the car and talked to Tommy as we ran down the logging road into the woods. About 300 yards into the woods I saw the jeep. Already men were putting a stretcher into a company truck. I glanced at the jeep and my heart sank. It was flattened across the hood and I could see where branches had been cut away from the passenger compartment. I had been praying all the way there, but after seeing this, I prayed, "Please, God, be merciful to John and his family".

John was unconscious and no one knew the extent of his injuries. "Has his wife been notified," I asked?

"No, sir, not to my knowledge", came a reply.

"Okay, Tommy, I'm going to Blue Ridge with John to the hospital. Please notify John's wife, Sarah, and call Helen for me".

"Yes, I will, Pastor".

The twenty miles to Blue Ridge seemed to take forever. John moved only slightly as he seemed to regain consciousness but did not make a sound.

Tommy called Helen, and by the time he got to the Mason's home, Helen was on her way there too. Somewhat surprised at seeing Tommy drive into the yard, Sarah, who vaguely remembered him from church, met him at the door. Trying not to startle Sarah any more than necessary, Tommy said "Mrs. Mason, there's been an accident. Mr. Mason is on the way to the hospital in Blue Ridge. Pastor

Slater is with him". Sarah's face turned pale as she burst into tears.

"Mother, what's the matter?" came a voice from the den.

"Your father has been hurt and is on the way to the hospital", Sarah said. About that time another car arrived. It was Helen. She asked Tommy to drive them to the hospital in our car.

The chill of the gray winter sky engulfed the four of them as they started for Blue Ridge. Helen was trying to console Sarah who was crying. Paula, likewise, had big tears in her eyes and was quietly praying. Helen suggested that they all have a prayer together. A few miles before reaching the hospital, Sarah broke the silence by saying, "Forgive me, Young Man. I forgot your name. This is our daughter Paula. We appreciate so much your driving us."

"You're very welcome, Ma'am. My name is Tommy Jones. It's nice to meet you Paula". Again there was silence.

Upon reaching the hospital, they entered the emergency room and spotted me sitting in the waiting area. I smiled at Sarah who burst into tears as they approached me.

"Be of good cheer. The news is good. John is okay. He was knocked unconscious when his head hit the steering wheel. He has no broken bones and no signs of internal injuries. The doctor wants to keep him over night for observation. If everything is okay in the morning, he can go home".

"Thank God," Sarah said as she, Paula, and Helen hugged each other. Tears came to Tommy's blue eyes as he shook my hand and said "Isn't God good to us?"

"Yes, He is, Tommy", I responded. The lonely searching I had noticed in his eyes when we first met was gone. In its place was peace and contentment.

It was quite late by the time John was taken to his room. Sarah stayed with John at the hospital. Paula went back to Stone Gap with Helen, Tommy, and me so she could get their car to pick up her Mom and Dad the next day. As we drove home, conversation was limited as if everyone were drained by the events of the evening and the lateness of the hour. It suddenly dawned on me that I hadn't been introduced to Paula. I broke the silence by introducing myself. Laughter filled the car and the strain seemed to diminish.

"I understand you're a nursing student, Paula", I said.

"Yes", she replied. "I have one more semester before graduation".

"That's great", Helen said. "I taught Home Economics and English for the last eight years before coming to Stone Gap. In the summer, I taught First Aid courses."

Paula's countenance seemed to brighten as conversation flowed more easily. I noticed Tommy glancing toward Paula several times, and with good reason. Paula was very pretty with unblemished complexion and shoulder length blonde hair. It's not always easy to make an accurate assessment of one's personality in only a few hours, but I had a feeling Paula possessed the same sweet personality and temperament her parents had demonstrated. I saw how level headed she was in the time we were in the emergency room. I saw her as she bowed her head and prayed silently. I took note of the respect she had for her mother.

The winding mountain road eventually brought us to the Masons' home. Because the hour was late and Paula had no one to stay with, Helen insisted that she spend the night with us. She graciously accepted and she and Helen went in to pack an overnight bag.

As Tommy and I sat in the car, I watched for his reaction as I said, "We need a nurse around here."

Quickly he replied, "Yes Sir, I think I'm feeling a little sick right here," as he placed his hand over his heart. That answered my question!!

As Paula came out of the house and toward her car, Tommy offered to drive with her to the hospital the next morning. She hesitated and then said "Yes, that's very thoughtful of you. Thank you, Tommy. Ten o'clock okay with you?"

"That's fine", he replied.

"Goodnight, Pastor, Mrs. Slater. Goodnight, Paula. I'll see you at ten", Tommy said.

Paula followed Helen and me to our house.

Tommy was up early. This morning he wanted to take care of the animals and other chores before he was to meet Paula. When Sue called the family to breakfast, Tommy was at the barn. Coming into the house, he told Alton and Sue what had happened the night before with the Masons. "I offered to drive the Mason's daughter, Paula, to the hospital today to pick up her Dad and Mom. I'm supposed to meet her at 10 o'clock. That's why I wanted to get the work done early," Tommy explained. Alton's eyebrow raised a little as he winked at Sue.

Paula had left our house early in order to go home and be ready to go with Tommy. Appearing very radiant, she hurried down the walk to her car as Tommy arrived.

"Tommy, will you drive?" she asked as she handed him her keys.

"I'll be glad to", he replied, as he escorted her to the passenger's side. As they started down the driveway she said, "I probably should have brought a scarf for my hair as windy as it is this morning".

"Oh, no, don't do that", came his reply. "Your hair is much too pretty to cover up".

"Why, thank you, Tommy", she said.

"Did you sleep well?" he asked.

"Yes, I did. I was exhausted after the ordeal yesterday. It turned out to be a pretty long day".

Then Tommy responded, "So you're a nursing student?"

"Yes, I am."

"How long will you be home for Thanksgiving?" he asked.

"I will be home for Thanksgiving and the week after," she smiled.

As they drove casually along, conversation seemed to come easily. Paula told how her father came to be transferred to the mill in Stone Gap.

"Do you have brothers or sisters?" Tommy asked.

"No, I'm an only child. Just Mom, Dad and me. How about you?"

"Three of us", he said, "Alton, my older brother, me, and Mary Katherine, our younger sister".

"Do they both live here?" Paula asked.

"Alton does. I live with him and his wife, Sue. They have four children. Mary Katherine attends college in Dahlonega."

Paula then asked about the children. Tommy told her about each one, their ages, temperament, etc., so fondly and descriptively, that it made Paula laugh.

"What is it?" He quizzed.

"Tommy, anyone listening to you describe the children couldn't help but know that you were totally devoted to them".

"Oh, I am", he said. "They're great kids."

Their morning together was so pleasant that neither was conscious of the time.

"Oh, Blue Ridge already?" Tommy sighed. "What time will they release your Dad?"

"They said not before 12:30 when the doctor makes his rounds", Paula replied.

"Well, it's a little after 11:00 now. Let's drive around the park", Tommy suggested. "It's always very scenic but especially this time of year. It encompasses two city blocks."

"It's beautiful", Paula replied. "I'd like to come back and sketch it and the old railroad depot when I have more time."

"We still have time for some coffee if you would like", Tommy added."

He couldn't believe the time had passed so quickly and he wanted more time to be with her. She smiled in agreement and then said, "Yes, that will be fine".

As Tommy came around to open her door, Paula, noticing his broad shoulders and gentle manner, became aware of a butterfly feeling coming over her. Somewhat surprised by this sensation, she blushed as he took her hand to help her out of the car.

A corner booth afforded privacy. The diner was not crowded this early, for which Paula was glad. Yes, the ice water was welcomed too, as she tried to regain her composure.

"Want something to eat?" Tommy asked.

"Maybe a donut" she replied.

"Okay, two coffees and two donuts", he told the waitress.

Time again seemed accelerated as Tommy and Paula shared that late autumn day. The easy conversation, the warm sun coming through the window, and their intense eye contact came to an abrupt end as they realized it was twelve noon. Tommy apologetically said, "The hospital is only a mile away". Paula was not displeased but a little embarrassed that she had lost track of time.

"Hi, Mom. Hi, Dad", Paula said. "You remember Tommy. He drove me over here this morning."

"Thank you, Tommy", Sarah responded.

After the normal greetings, Paula asked if her Dad were ready to go home.

"Yes, I am", he answered. "I'm ready for some of your Mom's cooking. Hospital food isn't all that good. The only thing we are waiting for is final release from the doctor."

A short while later came "you're okay to go home, Mr. Mason". With that welcomed news, they all left the hospital and started for home.

"Tommy", John said, "Sarah tells me you're the one who went for the Pastor when I was hurt."

"Yes, sir," Tommy replied, "I happened to come by right after the accident. The loggers asked me to call for an ambulance to meet them. Then I called Pastor Slater."

"I don't remember anything except seeing the top of a tree crashing down", John said. "When I regained consciousness, Pastor Slater was praying for me as the ambulance swayed from side to side on the curvy road. I want to thank you for all you've done."

"It's my pleasure," Tommy said as his glance met Paula's.

Arriving back at the Mason's home, John shook Tommy's hand. Then, he and Sarah went in leaving Tommy and Paula on the porch.

"Paula, I have enjoyed our time together," Tommy said.

"I have, too, Tommy".

He continued, "Will you be at the church Thanksgiving dinner?"

"Yes, yes, I will", she said.

Then he said goodbye and reluctantly walked to his truck. Tommy barely remembered leaving her driveway and was almost home when he faded back into reality.

CHAPTER 5

Thanksgiving day arrived with great excitement. Helen had given much attention to the details of decorations. She and the ladies had arranged bales of hay in various places around the fellowship hall accented by large pumpkins, corn stalks, and colorful chrysanthemums. Each table was decorated with small pumpkins and chrysanthemums as well. The pleasant smell of flowers and sweet hay made the atmosphere very festive. I enjoyed this holiday atmosphere and was having a great time sampling the food. I kept quoting the scripture to myself about *"not muzzling the ox that treads out the corn"*. (Deut 25:4 and I Timothy 5:18).

Eventually, the people started arriving. With each arrival, each face, each smile, joy swelled within me. Many children were there, each aglow with excitement and each a dynamo of energy. People came in cars, pickups, and two families even came in wagons, out of tradition rather than necessity. I noticed Al Jones taking Robin's wheelchair out of his car. How thankful he must be for his fine children. There was Tommy. Oh yes, and the Masons. I greeted them and told them how glad we were to have them with us. Things got kinda busy as others arrived.

Pa and Ma Mac were there. So were the Farleys, Caleb Fisher, Harry Chance from the store, and many of the good people I had come to know and to love. I guess I was the most thankful person of all. When it was time for lunch, I beckoned and the crowd became silent.

"A great feast awaits us today, and with joy we celebrate this day and partake together of this meal. Let us, in so doing, remember the ones who made this freedom possible and God who blessed us with the fullness of all good things. Our, Father, we thank you. We invite you to eat with us now as you have invited us to eat with you by the invitation you gave through your son, Jesus. Amen."

I backed away and watched my people converge on the feast at hand. Unconsciously, my desire for food was suppressed as I watched this scene. A feeling of utter joy and contentment gripped me as I caught a glimpse of Helen. She must have felt the same way for she was serving others with no apparent thought of herself.

I watched Tommy and Paula moving slowly toward each other and then heard Tommy telling her "I'm so glad you could come today." He was telling her about Alton's venison which Sue had prepared for this occasion . I could hardly wait to try it. Then my attention was diverted elsewhere. Something was tugging at my coat. As I looked down, I saw Robin.

"Aren't you going to eat?" she asked, with her little eyes questioning me.

"I wondered what that was pulling at my coat", I said. "You must be a 'Yankee' since you're always yanking at my coat". She giggled and I asked her if she would be my "Little 'Yankee'. She seemed pleased as she nodded yes.

By this time Sue and Ma Mac had pulled Helen away from the serving line and had prepared plates for us heaped high with turkey and dressing, venison, green beans, turnip greens, cranberry sauce, corn relish, and sweet potato pie for dessert. Sue prepared a plate for Robin, and Helen and I placed "Little Yankee" between us.

There comes a deep feeling of gratification when a celebration of this kind is totally successful in its intent. I was reminded of the five thousand that Jesus fed. How truly gratifying that meal must have been to Him who provided it, and to the twelve disciples who served it. I had not seen a visible miracle and yet I knew that God worked in a very real way. Only time would reveal what harvest would come from the soil that was tilled and the seed that was sown.

As any gathering, no matter how lovely and enjoyable must end, so this too, had to end. As the hum of conversation grew quieter, slowly our people began to disperse and a few cars at the time began to leave.

"Al, that venison was delicious", I said. "And Sue cooked it just right." Al seemed pleased and said "Maybe we could get another deer before Christmas."

"That sounds good to me," I replied.

"I don't know when I've enjoyed Thanksgiving as much as this one", Tommy said. "Paula you have made it special".

Not wanting to leave, Tommy hesitated and was about to say goodbye when Paula asked, "Would you like to come over to our house this evening and listen to some music?"

"Why, yes, if your parents won't mind", he replied. "I don't want to intrude".

"Of course not", Paula assured him. "About seven o'clock?"

"Yes, that's fine", he said.

Well, not just Thanksgiving evening but every day thereafter, either in person or by phone, Tommy made it a priority to make time for Paula while she was home. The day before Paula was to return to school, Tommy asked her to go riding with him. As they rode slowly through the countryside, Tommy began by telling her how he viewed his life.

"I grew up here", he said, "I've watched every season come and go, welcoming, yes, loving each one in its regular rotation. I grew up on the land. I took from it what I had to, and put back what I could." He slowly drove the pickup into a grassy meadow. He was silent until they got out and began walking. As he broke the silence, he stooped down and scooped up a handful of soil. "I am as much a part of this land as the grass or any flower or tree."

Paula, sensing the seriousness of the moment, took his hand. Pressing her hand into the soil in his palm, she was unable to speak. She was afraid she would offend by her reluctance to let him share his feelings for her, and afraid to make the commitment to look into his soul. As they stood there holding hands, she drew near him and lay her head against his broad shoulder.

"You're just a big teddy bear", she said. She kissed him on the cheek and whispered, "I think we had better go". He honored her request, and as they turned to go, a lump was in his throat, so he did not speak. His silence paid tribute to the feelings bottled up in him. Hers, too, was a silence for fear that she would say the wrong thing.

As they neared Paula's home, she broke the silence. "I go back to school in the morning. Will you call me sometime?" As she reached for the door to get out, Tommy gently but firmly pulled her over next to him and without a word, kissed her with such intense passion that it took her breath away. He walked her to the door and without lingering, said goodbye. Tommy left with the satisfaction that Paula fully realized his feelings for her.

The drive back to school was slow and sobering as the mountains, then the foothills, fell behind and faded away. With the change in the environment, maybe she could get a perspective on who she was, what had transpired these past two weeks, and where she wanted to go from here. She systematically tried to surpress the fond memories which inadvertently resurfaced. She must have time to analyze. Yes, that was it; she needed time to analyze. All that had happened was too fast, much too fast.

Burying herself in studies, Paula took little time to reflect on Stone Gap. At night, however, when things were still and quiet, she longed to hear Tommy's voice but he didn't call. First night, second, third, then the fourth night the phone rang.

"Paula, it's for you", her roommate announced. She dashed across the room almost tripping on the rug and grabbed for the phone. Then with a sigh of composure she said, "this is Paula".

Tommy was very matter-of-fact in conversation. He wanted to say more but couldn't. She wanted to hear more but wouldn't encourage him.

"Just wanted to see if you were all right", he said. "I wish you all the best, you know." Then after another minute of small talk, he said, "goodbye for now".

Now totally confused, Paula just stood there holding the phone with her mouth open. "If you would like to make a call, please hang up..." startled her back into reality.

"I wish you all the best? What does he mean, he wishes me all the best?!!" Was this a suggestion of finality, of closure?" This thought brought tears to her eyes. "What did he mean? Will he call back?" Two more days passed and Tommy did call back. Again, self-restraint on his part made him seem almost curt over the phone. Paula had never seen curtness in his behavior at all. He made a casual remark about the young people and children going on an excursion to hunt a Christmas tree for the church. After giving it a build-up, he intentionally omitted mentioning the date when it was to take place.

"Well, I'll go for now", he said.

"Tommy, what is the date?"

"The date for what?" he teased.

She said, "the date for the Christmas tree hunt!!"

"Oh," he replied.

He had baited her very well. He told her the date and, after a few more comments, said goodbye. She immediately checked the date for her final exams and happily found that they would be over by then.

CHAPTER 6

Christmas! Christmas, with cards, and lights, and carols, unmistakably comes every year. How is it that with all the heralds of its arrival, it manages to slip up on us almost without exception each year? I immediately thought of all the children. I especially remembered one little eight-year-old girl, and the first time I saw her, and the first time she yanked at my coat. Yes, I thought, Christmas must be very special for the children this year.

The last week of November had slipped by and I was amazed to realize that December had arrived so quickly. So much to plan and do... Besides all the planning for Christmas at church, I had sick people to visit. Also, a new family had moved to Stone Gap who had been at church last Sunday and I wanted to make a visit to their home.

The much-publicized Christmas tree hunt was threatened by a heavy snow that had fallen the day before. The thick clouds diminished and, though still overcast, the long awaited day looked like it would be fulfilled after all. The children had just gotten out of school for Christmas break and all were eager to get started. As announced, everyone met at the parsonage where Helen had prepared hot chocolate and cookies. Tommy had volunteered to bring his horses and sleigh when we knew we would have snow. He was tending the horses as everyone came into our home. He kept looking around and down the road until I finally persuaded him to come inside.

"Drink this. It will warm your insides", Paula said.

Surprised, Tommy said, "I didn't know you were here. I... I thought you hadn't come."

"Oh yes, I wouldn't miss this for the world", she replied. "I got home late last night from school. Dad dropped me off earlier so I could help Mrs. Slater bake cookies."

After a prayer we checked each of the small children to make sure their coats were buttoned, their hoods donned, and their shoes tied. Obviously, eighteen people couldn't all ride in just one sleigh, even a big one, so the smaller children rode and we larger kids walked. The new snow was fairly easy to walk through. It was about six inches deep and each step went crunch, crunch, as our gang laughed and sang across the meadow to the hills beyond.

Before reaching the wooded hills, we stopped to give everyone a breather and to check the small children, making sure they were still buttoned up. Each little red-nosed and cherry-cheeked youngster was radiant with excitement with the coming of the first big snowfall of the season, as well as with the Christmas tree hunt. At this point, some of the smaller children on the sleigh wanted to walk. Tommy helped them down and asked Paula, who had been walking with us, if she wanted to ride.

"Thanks, Tommy, but I think I'll walk with the children. I need the exercise".

Neither Helen nor I said anything but I knew that she was thinking the same thing as I. Paula, at times, had outwardly shown an interest in Tommy - nothing overwhelming, but a casual glance or smile. Now with the perfect setting and opportunity to be with him, she rejected it. Obviously, Tommy was stung by her refusal. After all, what about the friendly overture she had made with the hot chocolate only an hour ago? I was somewhat puzzled by her reaction.

The white meadow began giving way to a gradual uphill grade as snow-covered evergreens began to appear. They stood there, statues clothed in satin gowns with hints of emerald green peeking through. Around the trees were fresh tracks of rabbits and birds.

As we progressed into the woods, we came to a clearing and decided to make a base camp where we could have a bonfire. To everyone's surprise, Tommy had the forethought to have a big stack of firewood already cut and covered for our arrival. So, with not much effort, we had a roaring fire going in no time at all. We could make excusions out from the fire and return to get warm. Then when we selected a tree to be cut, we agreed to call everyone away from the fire and let each take part in the cutting. I took Robin on my shoulders and led about half the troop off in search of the perfect tree while the rest of the party kept the fire going and stayed warm. After scouting for about twenty minutes, I rounded up all the strays and headed them back toward the fire. I wanted everyone to have a good time but I didn't want anyone to get too cold. This time, Tommy led the remainder of the group, the warm ones, into the woods to search. Paula neither went with our group nor with Tommy's. She was not her normal, happy self. She just stood there with all the laughter going on around her and stared into the fire. Only an occasional snowball thrown her way pulled her away from her inner thoughts. I didn't know what was bothering her but something surely was.

A shrill whistle pierced the cold air. This was Tommy's signal that they had found a suitable tree. Everyone ran up the hill looking for the other group. I was glad Robin was no bigger than she was. Carrying only a few pounds uphill in the snow is very exhausting. As we topped the hill, we spotted the red caps and plaid scarves of Tommy's group gathered around a magnificent fir that was nearly ten feet tall. Tommy had done well. Each one, even the smallest child, was given the opportunity to hack away at the tree. The joy was not in the accomplishment so much as in the participation. I'm sure many memories were born on that simplest of days, each little hack making indelible marks in the minds of the participants. I watched Paula as she took her turn, stepped back, and stood beside Tommy. No words were exchanged. They just stood there, silent, motionless, like the snow-covered trees.

After each one had his turn, Tommy finished the job with a few solid chops. "I think I can get the sleigh up here and we can put the tree on it", Tommy said. That sounded good to me so while he went for the sleigh, the rest of us decided to look for holly with red berries, pine cones, and mistletoe to use for decorations. Everything being accomplished that we had come for, we started back down the hill. Our steps weren't as fast on the return trip, but all the joy was still there. The sprawling meadow lay before us now as we followed the path the sleigh runners had made earlier.

As the heavily laden sleigh cut its path through the snow and the rest of the gang staggered along, red faces glowed and excitement radiated while each breath puffed little clouds of vapor. With the whole world locked out and only laughter and the crunch of snow under foot, I drifted inside myself somehow overcome by the beauty and solitude of it all. What peace! With what instrument could it be measured? God surely must still the earth with winter and calm the weary pains of labor with this soothing blanket of white. I can only conclude that this is God's rest for his creation.

Strange, indeed! How rudely the realization broke into my mind that a trail of footprints crossed our own path and seemed to lead off to our right and up a small rise toward a remote valley in the distance. One man and one dog... How strange, indeed, for we had encountered no one and no other footprints on our way earlier in the day. "Tommy," I gasped, for by now the laborious walk, the bundle-some clothing, and the cold air were taking their toll on my energy. He heard my call and stopped the horses.

"Yes, Reverend Slater?"

"Tommy, let's rest a few minutes", I said. While Helen and Paula checked the children for mittens and scarves, I took Tommy aside and mentioned the other footprints.

"Yes, I saw them", he said. "A man and a dog".

"What do you make of it?" I asked.

"Well, from the direction and size of the tracks, one man and a dog, I'd say it was Ole Silas and Dog."

"It's Ole who?! And what?!"

"I think its Old Silas and Dog. Old Silas is sort of a hermit and Dog is what he calls his dog."

"A very appropriate name," I jested. "For a dog, I mean", as Tommy grinned at first and then both of us burst into laughter.

Tommy told me what he knew and what he had heard about Ole Silas. It seems that many years ago Silas had married and that his young wife, with whom he was very much in love since childhood, had died in childbirth. Since that time he had lived in seclusion and seldom came into Stone Gap except to buy necessary supplies. He was of mythical stature in the eyes of children and was the source of many bedtime stories. Tommy said he lived in a cabin at the end of a small valley about three miles away.

Again we started our Christmas tree gang toward home with new exhileration. "Ole Silas and Dog", I thought as we neared home…"a hermit, indeed?!"

Oh, calm, bright, lovely morning! Up a little later than usual this morning, I slowly walked to the window to look at the mountainside glistening in the morning sun. Well-used muscles were reminding me of the day before. Such a lovely scene I could see now, but such a lovely memory of yesterday. Perhaps this new day could be so lovely. I had scarcely finished shaving when the phone rang. Ma Mac was sick and running a high fever. I told Helen to forget about making my breakfast and that I had to go and pray with Ma Mac.

"Matthew, please take Daisy's canning jars back to her", Helen remembered.

There are times in a minister's life when he must go, must minister, even when his body rebels. Such was the case this morning with me. I was still sleepy and sore. You might say that my body was being just downright uncooperative. My car wasn't much better, but after three or four tries, it finally started. After all, it was 28° this morning. The warm air felt so good once the engine warmed up. Eventually, the fog of my own breath disappeared.

The road to the McHenry's home had no ruts in the new snow, so the going was slow. I could see several places where deer had crossed the road. Other than the animal tracks, the terrain flowed ever so smoothly as though the woods and pastures would engulf the roadbed. After a very slow drive, I arrived to find Daisy McHenry very sick and Aaron very much concerned. Relying on memory, sensing the urgency in Aaron's voice when he had called, I had rushed out and left my bible at home. I talked to them about the scripture *"where two or three agree as touching anything…it shall be done."* We prayed, we asked, we believed. I felt nothing; I saw no results. Aaron and I walked to the next room where a small fire was burning in the fireplace.

"A rough night for Daisy", Aaron said. "Thought she would be better by morning but she seemed to get worse. Sure am glad to have you here, Pastor".

We looked in on Daisy who seemed to be resting, and then we went back to the fireplace. Aaron and I had coffee and he asked me how the Christmas tree hunt had gone. I related all the little intricate details about the children's excitement as he clung to each word with gleaming eyes and a grin on his lips.

"Wish I could have seen it", he said.

"We're supposed to decorate the tree tonight after prayer meeting", I said. "It will be lovely. You and Daisy can see it Sunday if she feels up to it".

I had been there about an hour when we heard Daisy call. "Aaron, did you get Reverend Slater some coffee?"

We looked in on her again to find her feeling much better and the fever gone. I knew the power of prayer had done its work although I had felt no great spiritual emotion when we had prayed. We had a prayer of thanks and I prepared to leave.

"Reverend Slater, I baked some sweet potato pies. Take one home to Helen", Daisy called out.

"My favorite", I said. " I may let her have a small slice".

Daisy seemed pleased. They thanked me for coming as I started for the door.

"Please call me if you need anything at all", I said. "I'll look in on you tomorrow." On the way home, I kept smelling that pie and suddenly remembered it was about lunchtime and I hadn't eaten breakfast yet.

The evening was cold and the sky clear except for a few streaks of very high wispy clouds. Pleasantly surprised as we arrived at church for prayer meeting, we found that many folks were already there. Mid-week...cold weather, I thought. This was unusual to have so many people attend.

As we opened the service with <u>Joy to the World</u>, I became aware that the younger children's eyes were glued to the Christmas tree, as yet undecorated, standing near the front of the church. As they mimicked the words *"the Lord is come"*, their little eyes seemed to search each bough from the bottom to the top. I remember the excitement and wonder of being a child at Christmas. I knew instantly the theme of my Christmas message, "A Child at Christmas". After singing another carol, we had special prayer for Ma Mac and others who were sick.

With a blast of cold air, the door opened and John, Sarah, and Paula entered. I briefly mentioned John's accident and how thankful we were for his safety. I didn't elaborate. I thought that in time John might want to relate his miracle personally.

After more prayer and a few personal testimonies, I spoke briefly on why I think we decorate during the Christmas season. I summed it up by saying that when you drive down the road, you don't pay special attention to things unless you see a sign, a flag, or a light, particularly a flashing light or colored light. "Well, that's how it is with Christmas. It is so special that we hang colored, flashing lights and flags of silver and gold tinsel and bells and balls and remembrances because "Joy to the World, the Lord is Come"! With that, everyone stood and gave praise to God. I invited everyone to stay and help decorate the tree and then dismissed the service.

Helen and Sue had planned the refreshments. Jeff and Shirley Farley, having two children of their own, seemed to be the right choice to be in charge of the decorating. Everyone pitched in stringing lights, tinsel, and making ornaments. One ornament that had been hung on the back of the tree caught my attention. Almost hidden from view, I had seen Paula hang a praying hands ornament. It would be some time before we would learn its significance. With the lights and every ornament in place, everything was complete except for the angel. While Jeff and Alton held the ladder, I climbed up and gently placed the beautiful angel on top of the tree.

"Ned Benson, will you light the tree for us?" I asked. He seemed a little surprised but promptly plugged in the lights. While everyone admired the beautiful tree, I thought, " I'm not exactly sure why Ned is at church. He has not been since I came here as Pastor. Maybe it is the season that brought him." Although everyone knew him, there was in his persona an almost untouchable vagueness. Nevertheless, I wanted him to feel welcome. "We will not light the angel until Sunday morning", I said. "It's special."

"Refreshments", Sue announced. This was how I remembered Christmas. Refreshments then were a treat. We didn't have a convenience store on every corner where I grew up. Well, neither did Stone Gap. This made hot chocolate, popcorn, and Christmas goodies special. It was interesting to watch the reaction of people to stories, songs, and riddles. Alton made mention of how good the popcorn was. He said his grandfather was plowing his popcorn patch one very hot July day. He said it was so hot that the popcorn starting popping. The mule thought it was snowing, and lay down and froze to death!

A roar of laughter went up from everyone and then dead silence as Robin asked, "Daddy, how old were you then?" The roar was thunderous. I could hardly talk for laughing. After regaining partial composure, I glanced at Tommy, who was reaching for Paula's hand.

Sue told everyone that Alton surprised her on their first date. He had asked her if he could drive her to midweek service. She agreed but was curious as to why he wanted to pick her up an hour before service started since she lived only two miles from the church. "Well," she said, "It was a beautiful evening in late May and he came for me with a horse and buggy! It was a lovely ride and I realized why he came by so early."

Harry Chance, who owned the store and was normally the quiet type, spoke up by quizzing the kids. "Do you remember Noah in the bible?" "Yeah" they yelled. "Well, what was Noah's wife's name?" A brief silence followed as little brows furrowed and little minds searched for answers. Then Harry announced, "It was Joan...Joan of ark!"

"Awwh", groaned the kids; all of us kids! Harry then concluded, as he grinned at me and said, "I know I took a "Chance" telling that"!!

For a quiet guy, he certainly had a good sense of humor. We all had a great time and I wished Pa and Ma Mac had been there. I remembered that I needed to visit them the next morning.

After church, Tommy asked Paula if he could drive her home. She agreed and as they drove slowly along she told him about school and that she had been offered a position at a major hospital in Marietta upon graduation. She casually asked him what he thought. Not wanting to show the pain that such an idea brought, he just answered, "I wish you all the best, Paula, whatever you decide."

"There it was again...I wish you all the best!" There was silence for a while, then a sob. He knew she was struggling but he could only say "I would miss you".

Helen and I were up earlier than usual. There were only three days left to finish my Christmas message for Sunday morning and Christmas was only days away. Shortly after breakfast, Helen and I grabbed our coats and started toward the McHenry's house.

"What's in the bag?" I asked.

"Oh, just some goodies Sue and I saved for Pa and Ma Mac from last night", she said.

"What a sweet thought", I said. "But knowing you, I'm not surprised". Helen smiled. "A husband needs to make points when he can!" I thought.

Aware of our arrival, Daisy met us at the door before we had a chance to knock. "Come in, and welcome", she said.

Not surprised to see her up, but astonished to see her looking so well, I said, "You're looking much better today. Your face has more color in it, too".

"The Lord blessed me with healing and a good night of rest", she replied.

"She's looking better, isn't she, Pastor?" Aaron commented. "Pretty, too, but ornery", he chuckled as he came into the room.

"Better be nice, old man", bespectacled eyes gleaming as she reached for his extended hand. "Try to behave, we have company".

"Well, Pastor, how was the service last night, and did they get the tree decorated?" Aaron asked.

"Oh, the whole night was delightful. After a wonderful service we all decorated the tree together. Jeff and Shirley Farley supervised and Sue Jones and Helen were in charge of refreshments. The new family was there, the Masons".

"Wasn't that a Mason who was hurt in the woods the other day, Pastor?" Aaron asked.

"Yes, it was this same man, John Mason, who was at church with his wife, Sarah, and daughter, Paula".

"They're very fine people", Helen said. "Paula will graduate soon from nursing school."

"Will she live here?" Daisy asked.

"We hope she will," Helen replied.

"Pastor, tell us about the children - what about the children?" Aaron's eyes welled up.

Then Helen and I began to relate some of the stories that were told and how little Robin asked her Daddy how old he was when the mule froze to death in the popcorn patch. Aaron sat up on the edge of his chair, clinging to every word, staring into nothingness, as if he were seeing every scene. Daisy rocked contentedly by the fireplace, her white shawl draped over her shoulders.

"Pastor, how did the tree look?" asked Daisy.

"I'll let Helen describe it to you". Helen began to tell them about the lights, and the garland and the handmade ornaments. She told them that Ned was asked to light the tree.

"Ned Benson?" Aaron interrupted. "Good barber; moved here about fifteen or twenty years ago. He's a hard man to get to know."

"Well, you need to get to know him", Daisy blurted. "You need a haircut now!" She continued to rock. Aaron just grinned.

"She thinks I'm 'too' pretty when my hair is longer," Aaron said.

"Ummh", Daisy cleared her throat. Aaron winked at her and continued by saying that Ned had only been to church a few times since he came to Stone Gap. I made a mental note that I would do a follow-up with Ned.

"Folks, this warm fire and fellowship is great", I said, "but we had better go. I promised Helen I would take her to do some Christmas shopping. She told me she's making a list, checking it twice, to see if I've been naughty or nice."

To be perfectly truthful, she has checked it more than twice, maybe twice a day for the past three weeks. Helen was very attentive to details and very thorough. When we left Pa and Ma Mac's home, the better part of the morning had escaped. I knew we needed to conserve time since we had to drive into Blue Ridge to shop. Maybe I'm getting old but I like to be home by dark when possible. Twenty miles wasn't a long trip but it took almost an hour with all the curves in the road. With patches of light snow scattered throughout the wooded terrain, the warm late morning rays brought blinding reflections as we passed alternately from light to shadows, back to light.

I lowered my visor and asked Helen what she wanted for Christmas. I knew she liked jewelry so I had already bought her a gold ring with a sapphire setting before we moved to Stone Gap. I just wanted to keep her off-guard and surprised. She hesitated as her eyes filled with tears. "I want little Robin to be able to walk", she said.

Speechlessly, I drove on as I envisioned that lovely little girl whom I had grown to adore, standing, running, playing. "Understanding such things is hard", I finally said, "and explaining them, even harder".

Blue Ridge is a lovely town, very basic. Its very name inspires thoughts of mountain peaks and cold mountain streams. "Well, here we are", I said.

The streets had Christmas lights brightly shining and there was a nativity scene in the town square. Helen said she wanted to go to a department store first. I was reminded that it was only a few days before Christmas by the lack of available parking spaces. We had to circle the square more than once but then we spotted someone backing out.

"Pretty good," I said. "Within half a block of the department store."

As we walked past the lawn and garden shop we spotted Tommy Jones. "Hey, Pastor", yelled Tommy. "Hey, Mrs. Slater."

"Got your Christmas shopping done?" Helen asked.

"Most of it", he said. "I had to stop in here to get my chainsaw sharpened. Cutting firewood is much easier with a sharp saw".

After a few more comments we parted, and Helen and I made our way down the street to the department store. Opening the door, we were met with a medley of <u>What Child is This, Oh Holy Night</u>, and <u>Jingle Bell Rock</u>.

"Close your eyes and smell the fragrances of Christmas", I said. "What do you smell"?

Helen replied, "I smell leather, perfume, potpourri, candles...."

"What else?", I asked.

She took a deep breath and paused a moment..."candy, a variety of candy".

"Pretty good", I said. "All those scents but you can distinguish each one individually".

As we walked past the candy counter, I was taken hostage by the chocolate hazelnuts, chocolate Brazil nuts and chocolate covered cherries. You see, they all have a common denominator, CHOCOLATE! While I paid for the candy, Helen walked on ahead. I had to look up and down two or three aisles before I found her. I realized I hadn't remembered what she was wearing. How obvious are the things we don't see, I thought. I stopped, took out my notepad, and jotted down that thought.

Back on track again, I noticed Helen was talking with someone. It was Paula and Sarah Mason.

"How are you folks, today?", I asked.

"Very well," Sarah replied. She continued, "We really enjoyed the midweek service and decorating the Christmas tree. Paula tells me that she helped chop that tree. Is that true"?

"It certainly is", Helen replied. "Tommy Jones found a really beautiful tree and everyone from the youngest to the oldest took a whack at it. Eventually, Tommy finished felling it."

"Speaking of Tommy", I said, "we saw him down the street just before we came in here."

"Tommy?..." Paula exclaimed, and then blushed.

I continued with small talk trying to minimize her obvious embarrassment. After a few minutes we told them we were look- ing forward to seeing them on Sunday. Helen and I found our way to the clothing section and the Masons walked toward the front of the store. As they exited the store, Paula turned down the street.

"Our car is the other direction", Sarah said.

"I know, but I want to walk this way for a while", Paula replied.

"Okay, Honey", Sarah, agreed.

The thought of seeing Tommy had influenced Paula's decision to window shop at the hardware store, and then the lawn and garden shop.

"Mom, let's get some coffee and donuts", she said.

"Okay, Dear, that's sounds like an excellent idea to me."

As they were approaching the donut shop, Paula caught a glimpse of Tommy across and down the street. He was getting into his pickup. Paula was about to wave as Tommy backed out. Then she caught sight of someone else with him, someone with long brown hair. He seemed very attentive to her and, as they drove by, Paula could hear their laughter. They did not even look in her direction. Yes, it was a girl with him, a very pretty girl.

The possibility of seeing Tommy and the sudden rush of excitement after his name was mentioned had now become a hollow, empty feeling. "How dumb can I be?" Paula thought. "I've only known him a few weeks. But I thought he cared for me. How stupid of me! It's probably best...but I thought he really felt something for me!"

Sarah ordered two coffees and two donuts. "Cream and sugar?" asked the waitress as Paula emerged from her dismay.

"Mother, do you like living in this area; I mean in Stone Gap?"

"Well, yes, Honey. Your Dad and I have talked recently about the area and how much we feel at home here. Why do you ask?" Sarah continued. "Don't you like it here?"

"Well, yes, I guess I do. I don't know. Well, you know...when I graduate I have a job offer in Marietta. I've been thinking about that, and then coming here and meeting everyone..."

"Anyone in particular?" Sarah interrupted.

Paula dropped her head and tried not to show emotion. She felt her face grow hot as she tried to conceal her feelings which she was, as yet, unwilling to share with her mother.

Not wanting to pry, Sarah continued, "Don't you want your donut?"

"I guess I wasn't hungry after all", Paula responded.

Outside, the evening rays had begun to get lower. As Paula and Sarah walked in the shadow of the buildings, they pulled their coats more closely around themselves realizing how much cooler it had gotten. With shopping concluded, they started for home. Paula, glancing at the fuel gage, decided they needed to stop for gas.

"There's a station just outside town", she remembered. "I'll stop there."

Charlie's Quick Stop and Diner read the sign. Paula pumped the gas and went inside to pay. While waiting in line, she turned away from the counter and glanced around the diner. To her surprise, she saw the same girl she had seen with Tommy earlier. She was holding up a small brown teddy bear with a red bow. Paula was thinking what a beautiful girl she was and then realized that she was also looking at the back of Tommy's head. She listened intently and heard Tommy say something to the girl. She couldn't make it out but whatever it was, it made the girl giggle as she cuddled the fuzzy bear. And then, Tommy laughed out loud, too. As she stretched out her hand, the girl said "Oh, Tommy, It's a beautiful ring."

"Do you really like it, Katie?" she heard Tommy ask.

Paula paid for the gas and dashed out the door. This time it was more than she could control as tears rolled down her cheeks.

"Boy, it's cold", she said to Sarah, as she wiped her eyes and straightened her windblown hair. Very little conversation ensued on the way home. Sarah knew, however, that all was not well with her daughter.

Over and over came the visions of the beautiful girl who giggled as Tommy spoke. "I wish I hadn't stopped for gas at all", Paula thought. Just before reaching home she asked, "Mom, do you think it would be okay to invite Mark up here for the weekend and Christmas?"

"Yes, Dear, if you want to".

"Yes, that's exactly what I'll do," she thought.

CHAPTER 7

Mark Green was a veterinary student whom Paula had met in one of her chemistry classes about two years ago. Although they had gone to a movie and eaten out a few times, there was never anything serious between them. They, however, had become good friends. Paula had been the one to invite Mark to church where he eventually gave his life to Christ and became a devoted Christian.

When Paula called Mark to invite him up for Christmas, he said, "I'd love to come for the weekend, but I have to return on Sunday evening. Can you come back with me for Christmas?"

"Well," Paula replied. "I'll think about it". Not willing to commit, she thought about not being with her parents on Christmas day. After all, she was their only child. In spite of her hurt and pride and whatever other indescribable emotions she felt, she still wanted to see Tommy, to look at him, and see if there were a place for her in his eyes.

That night Paula lay in bed unable to sleep. She closed her eyes only to see Tommy's broad shoulders and calloused, yet gentle, hands that had held hers. How had she come to regard him so fondly and so quickly? She rolled over and tried to sleep only to remember "that girl", that giggling, bubbly girl, who obviously had Tommy's full attention. The teddy bear, the ring…"At least he didn't see me", Paula thought. "I didn't realize I cared so much". Anguish and crying eventually gave way to exhaustion as she sobbed herself to sleep.

The next morning, Paula awoke later than normal. She remembered the last time she looked at the clock was 3:10 a.m. Eyes swollen and still feeling physically drained, Paula made her bed. Then she washed her face, combed her hair, and tried to use make-up to conceal her obviously swollen eyes. After some effort, she felt a degree of confidence and made her way to the kitchen. Sarah, who was putting away some baking pans, greeted her.

"Good morning, Honey, want some coffee?"

"Yes, Mom, that would be great", Paula replied. "Mom, Mark is coming for the weekend but he said he has to return Sunday afternoon. He asked me to go back with him for Christmas."

"Do you want to, Dear?"

"Well, I don't know; I'm not sure yet," Paula replied. "Do you think Dad would mind? It would mean not being with you and Dad on Christmas day."

"Your father and I realize that you are all grown up now and have to make many decisions about your future. We want you whenever we can have you but we know we can't have you all the time."

"Oh, Mom," Paula cried as she hugged Sarah. "You seem to always have the right words when I need them. Thanks, Mom, I love you."

After getting dressed, Paula, feeling restless, told Sarah, "Mom, I think I'll drive to the mill and talk to Dad during his lunch hour".

"He would love that, Honey. You can take him a piece of fresh apple pie. That's his favorite, you know."

John Mason was as sound in spirit and personality as he was physically. His love of God and family coupled with a strong work ethic was rounded out by his good humor. As Paula drove the five miles to the mill, she breathed in the majestic country. The late morning sun shone brightly over the ever-rolling terrain. Overhead was an endless canopy of clear blue sky. "Nothing like this in Marietta," she thought.

Paula knew in advance how her Dad would respond. She knew his level-headedness and good judgment. "Hi, Dad. I thought I'd come to see you on your lunch break".

"What a nice surprise, Pinky", John replied. He had nicknamed her "Pinky" soon after she was born because she would point her pinky finger outwardly when grasping his hand.

"Mom sent you some apple pie."

"She knows it's my favorite", John said.

After some time Paula began. "Dad, what do you think of Marietta?"

"It's a nice place," he said. "Getting more and more crowded every day though...good people. What do you think of it, Pinky?"

"I agree with your summation", she said. "Dad, I've been offered a job in Marietta when I graduate. The time is not far off and I have to make some big decisions."

"What are your alternatives?" John asked. He wanted to be objective, open, and by no means forceful with his personal opinion. He had learned that one's greatest decisions ultimately are best made by that individual who has to live with them.

Nothing actually having been resolved, Paula made the transition. "Dad, Mark will be here for the weekend."

"Okay, seems like a nice boy", John went along.

"He has to return Sunday evening. He has asked me to go back and spend Christmas with his family. What do you think?"

"Nice boy", he replied being careful not to crowd her. "Is that what you want?"

"I'm not sure, yet, but I wanted to check with you first. Thanks, Dad", Paula said as she kissed him goodbye.

Somehow she felt better but she didn't know why. When she analyzed it all, she realized that John had not stated an opinion at all. "What a wise man", she thought. As she drove the five miles back home, something her dad had said kept reverberating in her mind...a nice boy, a nice boy.

CHAPTER 8

Sunday morning arrived at the Slater home with the excitement of another day in the house of God. *"Feed my sheep"* came the resounding mandate to minister wherever there was need. Today was different though. The words seemed to burn within me. Helen felt an air of excitement also.

"It's almost Christmas", she said. "Remember last year at this time? You were still working and I was still teaching. Remember how discontent we were?"

"Yes, I do remember", I replied. "We had more money, more security, more, more, more… but no real satisfaction. Every day we've been here has been a new, exciting day. I've never experienced such peace except when I accepted Christ as my Savior."

Helen smiled in agreement as she poured us more coffee.

"Honey, I'd like to be at church early this morning to greet all the folks as they arrive". Again she smiled and I knew she understood. And so we did arrive early this last Sunday before Christmas. I immediately adjusted the thermostat to make sure everyone would be warm enough. Then I plugged in the Christmas tree lights. After arranging my bible and sermon notes on the podium, I made my way to the door, and none too soon. Within five or six minutes people were driving up.

It was cold this morning. Everyone was bundled up to the point that it was difficult to recognize some until they removed hats, scarves, and coats. Aaron and Daisy were the first to arrive. I should have guessed that though after seeing the excitement in their eyes when we had last visited them.

"Aah! Look at that tree, Daisy", Aaron said with a broad grin.

"Give me a minute, Old Man", she beamed. "I have to wipe my spectacles. They're all fogged up." She took his arm. "Oh, yes, Dear, just wonderful!"

Then she confided to Helen that Aaron had proposed to her on Christmas Day.

Jeff and Shirley Farley were next to arrive with their two children. Both children were bundled up so much with heavy coats that they looked like penguins as they wabbled the snowy walk into the church. Underneath the caps, scarves, and mittens we discovered one little boy and one little girl excitedly chattering about Christmas and the snow.

Now the people were arriving in greater numbers.

"There they are", I thought as Alton and Sue Jones arrived with their family. "There was Alton, Sue, Little Tom, Betsy, Nathan, and yes, Robin". I saw Alton take her wheelchair from the car. We greeted each one and when Robin came by, she pulled at my coat. "Do you know who I am?" she asked.

"Of course, I do. You're my Little Yankee", I laughed.

Next came John and Sarah Mason followed by Paula and some young man.

"Pastor, I'd like you to meet my friend, Mark Green", Paula said. After the normal greetings, the Masons were seated near the front. The old saying still applies, "you have to come early to get a back seat!" Sure enough, the only seats not taken by now were near the front.

Starting time arrived before all the people had. As we made the normal announcements and prayer requests, others came in. One of the last to arrive was Tommy who obviously was embarrassed at being late. At his side was a very pretty girl. As they made their way to their seats, Paula's heart sank. As Tommy helped remove the girl's coat, her long flowing brown hair was revealed. Sitting down, Tommy glanced across the aisle, one row in front of him. There was Paula looking at him. He smiled at her. Then he saw Mark and the smile faded into a gaze. The congregation began, "*Joy to the World, the Lord has come…"*

"Who is that guy? She never mentioned him before!" Tommy thought.

"…And heaven and nature sing, and heaven and nature sing, and…"

"It came upon a midnight clear, that glorious song of old…"

" She is prettier than I remembered", Paula thought.

"…Of angels bending near the earth, to touch their harps of gold…"

"So this is Katie", Paula thought.

These thoughts and glances continued back and forth across the aisle throughout the singing.

"A Child at Christmas", I began. "A Child at Christmas…the very words inspire many different thoughts, thoughts that are as varied as the people who think them. May we all keep this in mind as we read from Luke 2:7-14:

And she brought forth her firstborn son, and wrapped him in swaddling clothes, and laid him in a manger because there was no room for them in the inn.

And there were in the same country shepherds abiding in the fields, keeping watch over their flock by night.

And low, the angel of the Lord came upon them, and the glory of the Lord shown round about them; and they were sore afraid.

And, the angel said unto them, fear not, for behold I bring you good tidings of great joy, which shall be to all people.

For unto you is born this day in the city of David, a Savior, which is Christ the Lord.

And this shall be a sign unto you; ye shall find the babe wrapped in swaddling clothes, lying in a manger.

And suddenly there was with the angel a multitude of the heavenly host praising God, and saying,

Glory to God in the highest, and on earth peace, goodwill toward men."

"Another Christmas story reads like this. *For God so loved the world, that He gave His only begotten son, that whosoever believeth in Him should not perish, but have everlasting life.* John 3:16."

"God's love is further explained like this; *For God sent not His son into the world to condemn the world; but that the world through Him might be saved.* John 3:17."

"Who is the world? The world is people, you and me. Now let's put that in perspective and it reads like this: For God so loved you and me that He gave His only begotten son that if you and I would believe in Him, we would not perish but have everylasting life. For God sent not His son into the world to condemn you and me; but that you and I through Him might be saved."

"What about a child at Christmas? God could have sent an adult. A child reflects innocence, love, and tenderness. He has neither preconceived opinions nor conditions for acceptance. Only a child has these attributes. Being born in such a lowly estate as a manger and wrapped in swaddling clothes somehow undermines man's baser natures such as pride, prosperity, and prejudice. The fact that lowly shepherds were the first to know of His birth is evidence that the Father intended for common humanity to be able to come to Him."

At that point, I flipped a switch I had mounted on the podium which lighted the angel on top of the tree. You could hear the hushed tones of excitement from the children and see the smiles on each face. After a brief hesitation, I continued:

"As we look around at our church family and the children in particular, how vivid are our thoughts as we relive memories, experiences, yes, and even dreams. We don't live in the past, but its experiences and observations enlighten us as we go through the present and into the future. *Glory to God in the highest, and on earth, peace, goodwill toward men.* Amen"

The sermon was well received and after the concluding carol, the presents under the tree were handed out. Many gifts of toys, candy, and a variety of other things were given to less fortunate children. Tommy was given one gift anonymously. As he opened it, he mused, "a mug with a miniature ax in it." He remembered suddenly that, in his haste to get to church on time, he had forgotten to bring a small present he had for Paula. "It wasn't much", he thought. "Anyway, she's with that guy".

With all the excitement of the Christmas season, many gathered around Tommy and Katie and exchanged greetings. Paula took this opportunity to quietly slip away. On the way home she thought to herself, "I guess my decision is made for Christmas."

"Mark, I think I *will* spend Christmas with your family".

Not quite sure what was happening, I had noticed the glances going back and forth all during my sermon. I related my observations to Helen on the way home.

"Looks like some fuel has been added to the fire", I said. Helen just smiled.

As Monday morning rolled around, Tommy started about midmorning to go into town for some livestock feed. He had deliberately left home later than usual in order to deliver Paula's present to her in person since he had forgotten it yesterday and she had left before he could talk to her.

"Good morning, Tommy, won't you come in?" Sarah asked.

"Thank you, Mrs.Mason. I just came by to see Paula. I have this small present for her and…"

"I'm sorry," Sarah interrupted. "Paula is not here. She left yesterday after lunch with her friend, Mark. She is spending Christmas with his family."

"Oh, …please tell her I came by."

"I certainly will."

"Thank you, Mrs. Mason. Maybe I can come by after Christmas before she goes back to college. I can give her the present then."

"I'm sorry, Tommy, but she is not returning here before she goes back to school".

"Oh," he said clearing his throat, "I didn't know…"

"May I leave the present with you?"

"Of course, you may", Sarah replied graciously. "I'm sorry you missed her".

"Thanks, Mrs. Mason. Merry Christmas."

Tommy drove slowly down the drive. "She's spending Christmas with Mark! Who's Mark? She never mentioned him!"

CHAPTER 9

This bright Monday morning I had determined to get a haircut. So many things to do this time of year... In the afternoon I would visit the local clinic and check on the sick. As usual, the community was well represented in Ned's barbershop. I made the normal greetings and sat down to listen and observe as I waited for my turn in the chair. It's always amazing to listen to the wintertime, "wood stove" farmers who talk of how tall the cotton will be this summer, and how many bushels of corn they can make per acre this year. It brings to mind the tales that fisherman tell...somewhat enhanced! I'm being generous with that analogy! An old-timer told how the corn one year was so thick and so tall that it blocked out the sun. "I thought it was evening and went home and ate supper at midday", he jested! I listened to one colorful character and scene after another as they painted the canvas of my mind.

As I got into the barber chair, Ned asked, "How do you want it, Pastor?"

I told him, "The sides just above the ear, and a little off the top. Just make me pretty".

Ned came back with "just above the ears I can handle, a little off the top, no problem; but making you pretty is going to take a while!"

I grinned a little and chuckled to myself as I watched the old codgers glance over the tops of their newspapers and reading glasses to watch Ned and me. Yes, they were all there; overall clad,

Union Made, Big Ben, Liberty, Lee; all icons of rural America. I thought to myself "I wish I had their collective wisdom and insight". Each continued his reading or "yarns" as the low murmer of conversation continued.

"Thanks, Ned."

He resisted at first my attempt to pay him, but I insisted on paying this time. I didn't want to appear to be a freeloader or to be lumped with those "men of the cloth" who expect such perks. Respect is not demanded; it is earned. Ned understood. He thanked me as I left.

"By the way, Pastor, mighty fine Christmas message."

The clinic was relatively small but well equipped and able to handle minor emergencies and short-term illnesses. People needing long-term care and surgery were transferred to larger regional hospitals. I looked over the list of patients to get a general idea of who was there. As I surveyed the waiting room, I took time with the kids. Some were waiting for shots, some were ill. One little boy told me they were going to shoot him. "Oh", I said. "You mean with medicine?"

"Yeah"! he said, "and then the lady gives me some candy."

"Well, that's just fine," I agreed.

One little girl asked me if I would stay with her until she had her shot.

"Okay, I will", I replied.

"Thank you for being so kind", her mother said. "She really has a fear of shots."

Where appropriate and welcomed, I encouraged the young mothers to bring their children to Sunday School. I have always believed that Sunday school is a vital link in Christian education. As children begin their formal education with kindergarten, so should they begin structured Christian teaching at that early age. Society often has a double standard leaving Christian education not addressed until puberty. By that time the church has lost seven or eight impressionable years; years lost to secularism in schools, media, and social environment. I still remember bible verses and chapters that I memorized as a very small boy.

Some moms were receptive while others were noncommittal. It

was encouraging when a few asked me to repeat the time for Sunday school. With that, I would give them one of my cards. There were not many patients today so after saying goodbye, I made my way to the parking lot. Tomorrow is Christmas Eve. I still have much to do.

The congregation was scheduled to meet at church at 7 o'clock to go caroling through the village. Plans were made, as well, to deliver food, goodies, and toys to those we knew to be in need. Ned Benson, Harry Chance, Jeff Farley, Caleb Fisher, Alton Jones, and Tommy all had their pickup trucks to transport the carolers and gifts. Harry Chance, in his quiet manner, had ordered extra sodas at his store and had brought ten cases to give away. Ned Benson had fifteen decorated tins of popcorn; Jeff Farley had many cases of canned goods; Caleb Fisher, the carpenter, had made many brightly painted toys, rocky horses, wagons, slingshots, and doll cradles. Alton, Tommy, and John Mason had spearheaded a fundraiser to provide cash to many who needed medicine or who needed help with utility bills. The church clothing bank had provided coats, sweaters, hats and mittens for all the children on our list. The ladies had baked pies, cakes, and cookies in sufficient quantity so that no one would be left out. Our beloved church secretary, Mrs. Chastain, had coordinated the list of needy families, carefully matching clothing sizes, gender appropriate toys, and other specific needs.

"Silent night, holy night; all is calm, all is bright..."

Each carol was cheerfully sung as the crisp night air carried the tones, not only throughout the village, but on into the stillness that extended into the hills. Radiant faces welcomed us at each house, as Christmas became a reality to us all. Where there was a predetermined need, we addressed that need as best we could. Children in tattered coats not only welcomed the toys and goodies but also a new warm coat. Mrs. Chastain had done a remarkable job.

Everyone was blessed that night, they and we. But two things stand out vividly to me. One was a small girl, maybe seven or eight years old, standing in the open doorway as we approached. While we sang, I watched her face change from one of sadness to one of joy. As she was silhouetted in front of the flickering fireplace, her little face beamed with hope as one who had received a cool drink of water in the desert. Just as vivid in my mind was the tenderness and love with which Harry Chance gave each child and parent a soda and made sure to leave them an extra one for later.

What a glorious night it had been. As we started for home, the thunderous silence engulfed us as the snow began to fall. Helen and I talked very little, just reflected on the evening and what it had brought. *"Silent night, holy night; all is calm, all is bright"*. Amen.

"What could compare to last night?" I thought, as I rolled out of bed that Christmas morning.

I had no family except some distant relatives. Helen had no family except one sister who lived in Phoenix, so Christmas here was very special with our church family. Helen was on the phone early talking with her sister. "Oh, Sis, I wish you could see my present from Matthew. He gave me the most beautiful ring! He made me open it last night after we came home from caroling." Then followed the full details of the ring and other gifts. "The area is so scenic here", Helen continued, " and now with the snow, it is even more beautiful. Matthew and I just love it. And the people… the people are so wonderful and warm."

I had to quit evesdropping and get dressed. Helen had given me a blue pen-striped suit, which I had just tried on when the telephone rang. We had gift-wrapping paper scattered all around the Christmas tree. Aaron and Daisy had promised to stop by before going to the Joneses. I had to make improvements both to the house and to myself before they arrived. The Farleys and their two children were having Christmas dinner with us at 5 o'clock. We had a pretty full day planned to which we eagerly looked forward. Everything this Christmas was like a dream. It was so wonderful that I was afraid I might wake up and find it not real.

CHAPTER 10

Paula and Mark were surrounded by his relatives. After all, this was Christmas Day. It was a tradition in Mark's family to always meet at Grandma's house for Christmas dinner. There was always lots of good cheer and lots of good food. Paula had been there before so conversation came easily. However, not feeling necessarily "chatty", she made her way into the kitchen to help with whatever needed to be done in preparation for dinner. Her thoughts turned inwardly as she took over the task of washing pots, pans, and utensils used in preparing the meal. "I wonder what Mom and Dad are doing...I wonder how the caroling went...I wonder if..."

At this point, Paula determined not to think about Stone Gap. She then became aware of someone touching her arm. It was Mark. "Come back to the den. You don't have to help with the chores, you're my guest", he urged.

"Okay, just let me finish washing these two boilers and I'll come in there", she replied.

As Mark left, Paula thought how nice he was. She remembered her father's words that day at the mill..."he's a nice boy, he's a nice boy". "He has a good family, one with values," she thought. "He's handsome, thoughtful, kind ...and *nice*."

After they had partaken in nothing less than a feast, the crowd segregated, according to mutual interests, into smaller groups - sports, politics, religion. Yes, that was about the right order. Aware that Mark had an interest in all three categories, Paula excused herself to phone her mom.

"Hi, Mom, how are you and Dad?"

"We're just fine, Honey, and how are you?" Sarah responded.

"I'm okay...I'm fine. We just finished a wonderful meal and, well...Mark's family is so warm. Mom, how did the caroling go?"

"Oh, Honey," Sarah exclaimed. "We had pickup trucks full of people bundled up. We had carols and snow; we had candy, sodas, food, clothing, and blessings for the needy. It was a glorious night."

With this description, Paula was overcome with emotion.

"Who all was there, Mom?"

Sarah hesitated for a moment, "Well, there was..." She began to go down the roll as she viewed them from her mental picture but before she could finish, a dam of emotion broke as Paula blurted out, "Was Tommy there?"

"Oh...yes, Dear, he was".

Not reserved any more, she had to know! Paula asked, "was he with anyone?"

"Why, yes, Dear," came Sarah's reply. ..."that girl with the long brown hair, you know, the one he was with Sunday morning."

Paula hesitated, not knowing what to think or what else to ask. The silence lingered for a moment when Sarah said, "Oh, yes, Honey. Tommy came by on Monday morning to see you. He was surprised and seemed disappointed that you had gone back so soon. He left a small gift for you".

Silence again. Then Paula said, "Thanks, Mom. I love you and Dad very much. Merry Christmas".

The Jones house was alive this Christmas with four children romping and playing with new toys. "Dad, when can you put our new swing set together?" Nathan inquired.

"After a while, after it warms up a little, Son", Alton replied.

"Everyone come to breakfast," Sue called.

A small stampede ensued and after everyone was in place, the blessing was asked. Alton concluded "and Lord, we thank you for Mary Katherine being home with us for Christmas. Amen".

"Children, eat your oatmeal first", Sue insisted. "Then you may have bacon and eggs".

"What did you think of the caroling, Sis?" Alton asked.

"Very lovely", she replied. "I remember most the glow on the children's faces, especially those who thought that Christmas and Santa had passed them by". Her voice broke... "When they saw the gifts, they exploded with laughter. ...just like when we were kids and Mamma and Daddy were alive".

A momentary silence fell over the table. Then, "tell us about when you were a little girl", Robin chimed.

Mary Katherine promised to tell them that evening around the fireplace.

"Tommy, why don't you ask Paula over tonight," Alton asked. "She seems sweet, good looking, too."

Tommy, not looking up, replied, "She left Sunday afternoon".

Alton realized he had touched a nerve and backed off with, "too bad."

Tommy finished eating and excused himself to go out and check on the livestock and gather the eggs. The snow crunched under his feet as he made his way to the barn. He wondered how things could have been so wonderful last night, and how he could feel so badly today?" Then he remembered that void he had felt last night as well. "I guess I'm dumb as a fence post to think a girl like Paula could fall for me. She couldn't wait to leave. I didn't even get my gift to her." A tear appeared and then another as Tommy, resting his head against the wall, languished in broken-hearted dispair.

Inside the house, Mary Katherine said to Sue and Alton, "I think he really cares for that girl".

"Yes, I think you're right", Sue replied. "I've noticed it for some time now."

Pulling Sue close to himself, Alton jested, "you're supposed to be noticing me".

Honk! Honk! Honk! came three blasts of a car horn. When *what to their wondering eyes did appear, but Pa and Ma Mac in that old station wagon here.*

The kids bounded out to the front porch as Sue, Alton, and Mary Katherine tried to keep up. Even Robin in her wheelchair got there ahead of them.

"Merry Christmas", Pa Mac shouted. "Merry Christmas"!

Then he began loading himself down with packages as if he

were carrying an armload of firewood. Daisy helped him as they all went inside.

"Come by the fire", Alton urged as Sue directed them to the den.

Daisy, still wiping her fogged-up spectacles, as she called them, cheerfully asked, "How are Nathan, Robin, Betsy, and Tom?" She recited them in decending order so as not to leave one out.

All the children hovered around Pa and Ma Mac. With Betsy on one knee and little Tom on the other, Aaron exuded love and affection seldom matched even between blood relatives. He and Daisy gave their undivided attention to the most minute query the children might come up with. Then young Tom felt of Aaron's beard and asked, "What do you have that for?"

Aaron chuckled along with everyone else, then quickly replied, "My face was so pretty I had to cover part of it up so Daisy could stand it. I didn't want to be *too* pretty".

"Um..." Daisy grunted, looking over her spectacles at the children.

They all burst out with giggling as Alton and Sue continued to share their family treasure with Aaron and Daisy that Christmas morning around the fire.

Uneasy with the fact that Tommy had been gone so long, Mary Katherine went outside to see about him. She followed Tommy's tracks to the barn and cleared her throat before entering. Tommy was giving hay to the horses.

"I was missing you", she said . "Pa and Ma Mac are here with presents for the children."

Tommy didn't immediately look at her. He was a little embarrassed. She offered to gather the eggs. She knew he had been crying and didn't want to show it. They continued to talk as she collected the eggs.

"Okay," she said. "I'm finished. Come on in the house and I'll have some hot chocolate ready. It will warm your insides".

"That sounds good," Tommy, said, somewhat boosted in spirit.

Mary Katherine then made her way back to the house. Tommy remembered, "...It will warm your insides". Where had he heard that? That thought resounded in his mind repeatedly as he rejoined the family.

Tommy greeted Pa and Ma Mac with fond familiarity. Mary Katherine served hot chocolate to everyone and when she handed Tommy his mug, a light came on in his head. <u>Paula</u>, Paula had given him hot chocolate and said, 'It will warm your insides'.

Joy and pain mixed as he relived the scenes from only a few days before. "She's the one who gave me the mug under the tree at church. What a strange girl!"

The children's eagerness to open gifts took preference over conversation. "Well, I reckon it is time for presents", Aaron agreed.

Aaron and Daisy smiled with pleasure as each child opened his gifts. Tommy put his arm around his sister's shoulder as he told the children that Pa and Ma Mac used to bring Christmas presents to them when they were children. With that, Aaron presented Tommy with a gift while Daisy presented Mary Katherine with one. Daisy had crocheted a lovely shawl for her. To Tommy's surprise, Aaron had gotten him a sharpening file.

"I understand you pretty well used your axe cutting the Christmas tree for church", Aaron said. "Well, I thought you needed something to keep it sharp".

A gleam came in Tommy's eyes. "Yes sir," he said gleefully, "I really do".

Tommy could barely resist the impulse to shout out loud, "And that explains the axe in the mug. Oh, Paula, what a strange and wonderful girl!"

The Jones family had by no means forgotten to have gifts for Aaron and Daisy. Even the children had made drawings or cards or cutouts for them. And, of course, Sue had reserved a Christmas picture of the children for them. Pa and Ma Mac left that Christmas day carrying presents and loaded down with love and laughter... not a heavy burden to carry.

That evening after supper, Mary Katherine made good on her promise to tell the children about when she was a little girl. Each tooth-brushed and pajama-clad child snuggled up around the fireplace. And so began "once upon a time, when I was a little girl..." She told them that when she was little, she used to follow Uncle Tommy around and do whatever he did. "One day, I saw Tommy hanging on a tree limb by his legs, up-side-down. It looked so easy

I thought I would try. Well, I did try it but when I got up-side-down, I couldn't get up again. After hanging there a while, Uncle Tommy rescued me.

Another time, I had wanted to catch a baby pig and play with it. I caught the pig all right, but when it squealed, the mama hog chased me out of the hog pen."

Little eyes widened as furtile imaginations soared. She continued, "My Mama and Daddy, your Grandmother and Grandfather, used to gather your Dad, Uncle Tommy, and me around the fireplace like this and have devotionals, bible quizzes, and tell us fairy tales." At their insistence, Mary Katherine started with <u>The Three Little Pigs</u>, then <u>The Three Bears</u>. By this time the day's activities had taken their toll and four little ones were asleep.

After the children had been tucked in, everyone else followed suit shortly thereafter. Mary Katherine's fond memories took her back to her childhood Christmases.

Alton finished his day by saying to Sue, "Honey, I can't figure out why Tommy was so excited about getting a file!"

Before falling asleep, Tommy thought about his Christmas mug. He was puzzled by Paula's apparent sentiment as shown by her gift to him, and yet, there was the appearance of Mark from out of nowhere. Then there was Paula's rapid retreat from church without even speaking to him. "With Mark for Christmas, but why?! Why no explanation?" As he lay there in the dark that cold winter night, Tommy realized how lonely he had become and that when Paula was near, she dispelled that loneliness.

Ninety miles away Paula, unable to sleep, was envisioning broad shoulders, gentleness, and piercing blue eyes embodied in one named Tommy. Even though it was only a few weeks ago they had met, she felt as if her soul had merged with his. "This former stranger, how could it be? And then for him to rip apart her heart by casually seeing another girl after acting like he cared. He even brought *that girl* to church. He has his nerve"!

As caring turned to hurt, and hurt to anger, and anger back to hurt, the vicious cycle continued until she sat up. "I wonder what he got me for Christmas? What time is it? I could have Mom open it for me. Oh, no, it's after midnight! Nothing to do but sleep. After all, sleep is the antidote for pain". As she lay there, the numbness of sleep overtook her tortured mind as happier scenes of rolling hills and late autumn days, scenes of oneness with another, delightful days with Tommy, flooded her unconscious mind.

CHAPTER 11

Two days after Christmas I felt a nagging, ridiculous compulsion to hike into the valley of Ole Silas and Dog. I told Helen of the driving force behind my decision to venture afield, this day of all days. After assuring her that I would be okay, I asked her to pack a bag of goodies and a loaf of freshly baked bread to take to Ole Silas. I dressed for the occasion and told her that I would be home by four o'clock at the latest.

"It is 9 o'clock now. If I'm any later than 4 o'clock, call Tommy and tell him I started up the valley at the spot where we saw the tracks while returning from our Christmas tree hunt".

Helen knew that I was a good woodsman and knew how to take care of myself, but she was still apprehensive. Handing me a white canvas bag full of goodies, she kissed me and reluctantly said goodbye.

"No later than four o'clock", she said as I trudged off through the snow.

I had planned to make this missionary journey at some point. I just didn't plan to make it this soon, and in six inches of snow. Upon reaching the spot where the trails intersected, I turned up the valley toward Ole Silas and Dog. I didn't know what to expect. I didn't know much about Ole Silas except what Tommy had told me. I had gone about two miles when the valley began to narrow and the trees grew thicker. Lost in thought and solitude, I was startled back to consciousness by a crashing sound in the brush. I froze in my tracks, nothing moving except the hair standing up on the back of my neck. Then suddenly a 10-point buck bounded over a log and vanished.

I glanced at my watch and saw that it was 10:20. After about another mile, I could tell that the cold and the stressful walking in snow were sapping my energy. I decided to stop for a while and rest. Finding a big log on which to sit, I laid the goodie bag on the snow beside me. After a candy bar and some water from my canteen, I rested briefly, and then continued on my mission. I had gone about 300 yards further up the trail when it ended.

The valley was thicker with trees and narrower. I decided to stay in what I considered to be the center of the valley. A small stream meandered from side to side across my path causing me to have to cross it repeatedly. TRACKS! FRESH TRACKS! BIG TRACKS! One man, one dog. Again I felt that same funny feeling on the back of my neck.

While resting on that log, I had the feeling of being watched. I think now that I was right. "I'll do the obvious thing," I thought; "I'll follow the tracks". Wrong!! Within 200 feet the tracks faded out, or rather had been brushed out. "Well," I thought, " the tracks had to come from somewhere". Armed with this logic, I returned to the spot where I had first come across the tracks. I marked the spot and from that point I followed in the direction from which they had come. What seemed like an hour, but actually 20 minutes later, I broke into a clearing. There, maybe 100 yards away was a rustic cabin with a stream and small waterfall behind it. A well-supplied reserve of firewood was neatly stacked on the porch. Another stack extended out from the cabin on the other side.

A short distance across the yard, I became aware of two well-kept graves, one large and one small. Each had a rough-hewn head-stone. "Strange", I thought, "a third headstone but no grave". Behind the headstones were flowering shrubs which appeared to be camellias. Their red-rose colors were interspersed with snow which had fallen during the night. With evergreen leaves for background, they paid tribute to love still alive as they kept a vigilant watch over the fountain of that love.

I stood there about ten minutes resting and collecting my

thoughts. I knew at this point, I was being watched by man and animal. Not wanting to intrude further, I decided to hang the bag of goodies from a tree limb near the edge of the forest where I was standing. I then retreated into the woods and backtracked to the spot I had marked. I left, not out of fear, but out of respect. I felt that my mission was accomplished for today, but there would be another day. As the valley widened again and the view broadened, I joyously headed for home. Yes, I felt assured that God's will had been accomplished this day and that, most assuredly, there would be another day.

CHAPTER 12

The Anderson boys - the very mention of their names made folks around here stop and take notice like the words *interest rates* do on Wall Street*!* The only thing they liked to do better than drink and fight, was to fight and drink. Throw in a noisy red Ford every now and then and you've pretty well gotten the picture. "Hell-raisers" they were called. It was easy to see why!

The week between Christmas and New Year's, Benjamin and Bartholomew Anderson were arrested in Blue Ridge for drunkenness, brawling, and disturbing the peace. The only thing that saved them from a DUI charge was the fact that they were arrested before they could get to their car. These boys really love to fight…they were fighting each other!

I had been introduced to them briefly through community visitation. They weren't very receptive or, for that matter, very friendly. At the request of their widowed mother, Millie, I said that I would try to intercede on their behalf. It was around lunchtime when Mrs. Anderson called. I asked Tommy if he would accompany me to see the boys and he agreed to go. On the way to Blue Ridge, he gave me some background information on them.

"The Andersons used to be in church regularly until about ten years ago when Mr. Anderson died of a heart attack. Mrs. Anderson had to pick up the load by herself. She had to start working shifts and weekends. Her church attendance became less and less. The twins had to be left by themselves many times. They seemed to get more and more rebellious until things got out-of-hand."

Armed with that knowledge, my frustration with them became diluted by compassion and understanding. "It really helps to understand the problem," I remarked.

Upon entering the jail, we could hear the drunken shouting and profanity. We asked for the officer in charge of the Andersons. When the officer came out, it was an old school buddy of Tommy's.

"Pastor Slater, this is Bob Camp, an old classmate of mine".

"Watch out now Tommy", Officer Camp retorted, "not too old". Bob Camp was very congenial and offered to help in any way he could.

"Bob," I said, "I want to ask for your special indulgence. Can you arrange with the proper authorities to have the Anderson boys released into my custody for a probationary period of thirty days? If they get in trouble, I'll take full responsibility. If they mess up, I'll go before the judge in their place."

"Pastor, I'm willing to try but do you know what you're letting yourself in for?"

After some time and probably much effort, Bob obtained the proper authorization from the Judge for their release. Then he took me back to the cells to let me observe them.

"Bob, when do you go off duty?" I asked.

"At 8 o'clock p.m.," he said.

"We will be back by 6 o'clock to get them."

"Yes, Pastor. That's fine with me", Bob said.

It was 3 o'clock by now so I asked Tommy if he could stay. He said he could and suggested we go to a diner which was nearby since we had not eaten lunch. Charlie's Quick Stop and Diner was the choice.

"I often stop here when I'm in Blue Ridge", Tommy said. "They have very good coffee".

Tommy and I talked about the Anderson boys and I remarked, "What a blessing to the community it would be for them to turn their lives around and become productive instead of destructive". We talked about Christmas past and the New Year. We talked about what would be planted this spring, about Robin's condition, about the Masons, and John's miraculous escape. I asked him if he had heard from Paula. He wouldn't look at me immediately. I assumed that he thought I might read the anxiety he felt at the mention of her name.

"No, Sir, I haven't".

That's all he said.

"Tell me," I asked, "how old are the Anderson twins?"

"Twenty, I think," he replied.

After more conversation and too much coffee, it was 5:30.

"Tommy, I have taken your whole day. Let's go over and see what those *good ole boys* are up to."

Back at the jail, I asked Tommy to wait with Officer Camp while I went back to visit the Andersons.

"Hello, boys", I said.

"Whada ya want?" one snarled.

"Do you know who I am?" I asked.

"Yeah, you're that preacher".

"Boys, I want to tell you a true story and then I'll tell you how you can go home today." With that prospect they listened up. I began:

"We were all born in sin, every rotten one of us! All were bound for hell. Someone had to buy us a get-out-of-hell free card. Jesus bought that card for us and has offered it to everyone who asks for it. That is called salvation."

"Yeah, Preacher, we've heard all this before", they barked.

"Oh, I'm sure you have. You just haven't been smart enough to take advantage of it", I said. They seemed shocked by such a stern reply. "The devil came to steal, kill, and destroy. Christ came to give life abundantly. That's all I have to say".

"Okay, okay - now how about us getting out of here today?"

While I was at the diner I had cut out two index-sized cards from a cardboard box. In bold marker I had inscribed- ONE GET-OUT-OF-JAIL FREE CARD. I held these cards up so they could read them.

"Are you kidding us?! Get out of here, Preacher!"

"I know it sounds too good to be true, but these are your get-out-of-jail free cards; one for each of you. Before you respond, let me tell you the conditions you must meet."

They just stood there peering through the bars at me in disbelief.

"You men are to be released into my custody for a period of thirty days. You will be accountable to me for your activities. You will not drink! You will not fight! You will not drive in an offensive manner!"

"Yeah, and we'll be in church three times a week", one mocked.

"Oh, no", I continued. "No church will be required. One more thing, however, will be required. Each of you will read the book of John on a systematic schedule and will answer questions on what you've read. If you accept these cards, you also accept these conditions. Any breach of these conditions by either one of you will land you both back in jail; this I promise you."

I think my sternness and this sudden realization of accountability boggled their minds.

"I'll leave you men for a few minutes to talk it over", I said.

I gave them fifteen minutes and then went back in with the conditions typed in duplicate, thanks to Officer Camp.

"Well, Men, what's your decision?"

Ben said, "Pastor, we accept your conditions".

"Bart?", I prodded.

"Yes sir, I do too".

I had each one sign and date his copy of the conditions, giving each one his copy and keeping the duplicate. I then handed each of them his card and called for Officer Camp to open their cells. They walked out free but not belligerent, not haughty, not cocky.

As we exited, I told Ben and Bart that I had asked Tommy to come with me.

"Hi, Tommy", they said.

"Hi, Guys", he replied.

"Tommy, Ben and Bart are free to go", I said. "Men, can we give you a ride?"

"Yes sir, our car is in the police impound yard."

Only a few blocks away, I drove them to the impound yard. When I went inside to make arrangements to get their car released, Ben asked Tommy, "What kind of preacher is he anyway?"

"He's the kind of preacher who promised a Judge that he would take your penalty if you messed up."

"Men, here are your keys. Do you have money for supper and gas?" I asked.

"Yes sir, we do, and thank you", they responded.

I shook hands with both boys and told them that I would contact them the next day. Tommy and I drove on ahead of them, not wanting to give them the feeling of being watched.

"Stone Gap looks very good indeed," I remarked to Tommy. "It's been a good day's work. Thanks, Tommy, for going with me."

I related to Helen everything that had transpired as we sat eating a late dinner. "I believe those Anderson boys can be reached", I said. "Helen, will you go with me to visit Millie, their mother? She has been widowed nearly ten years. She has to work and care for those boys all by herself". I told Helen everything that Tommy had told me.

"Poor woman", she sighed sympathetically.

"I'll contact Mrs. Chastain and get all the information I can about Millie and what her schedule is".

After a good night's sleep I was refreshed and felt that I could deal with Ben and Bart with a much clearer head. I found out that Millie would be home Saturday morning so I decided to see the boys alone this afternoon.

I was fully expecting some test of my resolve or some scheme whereby they could circumvent the agreed upon conditions. To my surprise, I found them both at home expecting me. I was determined not to let my doubts surface. Bart let me in to a simple but clean house. I saw none of the things which one would expect to see in the home of such notorious "hell-raisers".

"Well, Men, how are you feeling today?" I began.

Ben offered me a seat. "Oh, pretty well", said Bart, sporting a black eye as he shook my hand. Ben offered to shake my hand but flinched, and then I noticed his swollen hand.

"Looks like you hit something pretty hard," I said, glancing at Bart's eye.

"Men, do you have jobs?"

"Well, off and on", they replied.

"Do you work days or nights?"

"Day time", they said.

"Good", I continued. "Now this is what we will do. You will report to me every Monday, Wednesday, and Friday, one of you at 5:00, the other at 5:30. Today is Thursday so starting tomorrow, I want to see you in my office at church. I see you have a bible so start reading the book of John in the New Testament. Read chapters 1 through 3 and we will discuss them. I will keep an ear open for any disturbances which may occur between visits".

I wanted to treat them with respect but with firmness. I knew that like fishing for a bass, you had better keep a tight line or he will find a way to get loose! I didn't linger or badger or pray. I just shook their hands and left.

When I returned home Helen's eyes were red as she hugged me. "I knew you would be praying for me", I said.

"How did it go, dear?"

"It's going to be a slow process but I think it will work", I replied. "I start their therapy tomorrow at 5 o'clock at church."

I wanted to get a jump on the weekend and any activities they might be drawn into. Then there is New Year's Eve with all the usual drinking and reveling. " Got to pump God's word into them before then," I thought.

Friday morning found me praying about my first session with Ben and Bart. "Lord, let me relate to them and them to me. Don't let our age difference be a barrier."

I read and reread John chapters 1 through 3 to glean as much as possible. I wanted to help them understand the love of Jesus and the simplicity of salvation. I was back in my office well before 5 o'clock. I had made a chart on each of the boys in order to mark his progress. At the top was a check-in time. I wanted to measure their punctuality, an indication of their seriousness. At 4:55, I heard a car arrive. I knew from the glass-packs that it was the twins.

"Ben couldn't make it today", Bart announced, "but I'm here."

"I'm sorry, Bart. The conditions were for the two of you. It's two or none."

"I'll try to find him," Bart said, "but what if I can't?"

"Its two or none; period!" I affirmed.

Bart quickly departed as I listened to him drive off. I figured they were trying me, "stretching the envelope", as it were. The parameters having been set, I didn't intend to budge from my position. In twenty minutes I heard the car return. This time Ben came in.

"Sorry, Preacher, I'm a little late. I almost couldn't make it. You see, I ran into the door and busted my lip", he said as he wiped blood from his mouth.

"Oh?" I said. I knew what he had run into was Bart's fist. And so we began by discussing who John was, and his relationship to Christ. We discussed that John was eminently qualified to tell of Jesus because he was so close to him and knew him so well.

"How well do you know Bart?" I asked.

"Better than anybody except Mom".

"Why do you know him so well?"

"Because we eat, sleep, work, and ..." He started to say, fight, but checked himself.

"Well, that's how well John knew Jesus", I said. "Ben, read John, chapter 1, verses 11 and 12".

He read, "...*He came unto his own, and His own received Him not. But as many as received Him, to them gave he power to become the sons of God, even to them that believe on His name*". "I want you to memorize those two verses by Monday and be ready to recite them. Now, let's look at John 3:16 and 17."

"I remember them from Sunday school, Mrs. Chastain's class", said Ben.

He then recited them verbatim. "That's good, Ben." I said. "That's all for now. See you Monday."

I used the same format with Bart. Both boys surprised me with their reading skills and intellect. Hurdle number one was passed. Only time would tell how well they would respond to this regimen.

The next morning was Saturday and Millie Anderson was at home. Helen had managed to talk with her Friday afternoon and she agreed to see us. As we arrived at her home, I noticed the absence of the boys' car. I was glad they weren't there. We would have more freedom to talk openly with Millie without them. Millie was an attractive lady, maybe fifty years old. She was very neatly but conservatively dressed.

"Please come in, Rev. and Mrs. Slater", she said. "May I take your coats? Please be seated. Would you like something to drink"?

"Thank you, no, but maybe later", I replied.

Before I could begin, Millie said, "Rev. Slater, I want to thank you for what you did for Ben and Bart. I really appreciate it. Those boys have been a handful lately."

"They are such bright and good-looking young men. Tell us about them", I said.

She began. "When their father, whom they adored, passed away nearly ten years ago, they seemed to turn bitter. I think they blamed God for their father's death. It was so hard for them to understand how God could take their dad, the dad who always took them to Sunday school and church. Then I had to start working shifts to make ends meet. The boys had to be without a father or mother many times. Without anyone here, they just went their own way. I'm not making excuses for bad behavior. I'm just telling you how it was."

"Millie", I said, "the Judge has placed the boys in my custody for a thirty-day probationary period. I am working with them separately on Monday, Wednesday, and Friday." I told her the conditions and what was expected of the boys. She cried and smiled. "They have needed someone to be accountable to."

Then Helen asked gently, "Millie, what about you? Do you have friends or family or neighbors, or someone to help you?"

"Not to speak of", she said. "Oh, I have a few friends, not close though."

"Millie, the church needs you and welcomes you", Helen continued.

"Those people are so nice. I remember Mrs. Chastain used to teach my boys in Sunday school". Millie began to cry. "Mrs. Chastain called or came by probably a dozen times after we stopped going to church. So did other people like the Joneses, the McHenrys, and…" She broke down and really poured out her heart. "I guess I became bitter, too, but didn't know how to handle it."

"Millie, please come back and let church be a part of your life again," Helen pleaded. "You'll find Jesus right where you left Him".

Millie groaned with emotion. Then while she was sobbing, Helen and I prayed quietly with her. She looked up as a radiant smile replaced her weeping. When she regained composure, she enthusiastically asked, "How about some coffee now?"

"That would be great", I said.

We talked about a lot of things in general and then Helen zeroed in on the ladies group at church. "We'd love to have you attend", Helen said. Millie was very receptive to the idea although she didn't commit.

"Millie", I said, "we have enjoyed our time with you. Thanks for the coffee".

Helen hugged her and we left. As we drove home, Helen cried. "How sad - a woman alone, trying to raise two boys by herself. I hope we can be friends to her".

CHAPTER 13

Paula could stand it no longer. No classes till January 6th and here she was with all this time on her hands, and nothing to do but think. And thinking, right now, was painful. Her unanswered questions were starving for answers.

"I'm going home! If nothing else, Mom and Dad will be glad to see me."

She threw herself across the bed finally admitting to herself, "Tommy, I love you; I love you so very much". She felt better just saying it, finally verbalizing it. "I'm going home!"

With tears streaming down her face, she quickly packed her bags and dialed home. "Hello, Mom, I'm coming home. I'm leaving now. No, nothing is wrong, I'm just coming home".

It was early evening before Paula reached Stone Gap. Passing by the church, she thought of the last time she was there and saw Tommy with "that girl". But she would not think of that now. "I could call and let him know I'm back. No, I'll just wait until tomorrow morning and see him in church".

"Hi, Mom. Hi, Dad. I guess you're surprised to see me back so soon."

"Not surprised, Pinky, but very pleased", John said, hugging her.

"Yes, Dear, it's good to have you home", Sarah added.

After a respectable amount of time with her parents, Paula excused herself. She couldn't wait to open her present from Tommy. Slowly untieing the ribbon and carefully unwrapping the box, she saw a small teddy bear. She immediately thought of <u>Charlie's Quick Stop</u> where she had seen Tommy and "that girl" and, oh yes, a teddy bear. But wait; there was something else in the box. It was a beautiful friendship ring. "A very sweet thought", she said. "I guess we are friends". Paula knew in her heart that she wanted to be much more than friends.

Sunday morning found Paula up early making sure her clothes looked just right. She took more time than usual with her makeup and every hair had to be in place. Not wanting to be late and to be ushered to a seat near the front, Paula suggested to her parents that they leave for church a little earlier that usual. John grinned at Sarah and winked.

The Masons did arrive early and were seated about five rows from the front. Though anxious to see who came in, Paula was reluctant to turn around. She relied mostly on what she could see out of the corner of her eye and on whose voices she could hear. The congregation was gathering in rapidly now as the low sweet tones of the organ began reverently playing "Amazing Grace." Paula became aware that the pews in front and behind were filling up.

"Over here, Uncle Tommy", came a child's voice behind her. Without thinking, Paula's head snapped around to see Tommy being seated on the pew behind her. He smiled, obviously surprised at seeing her. And "that girl" was with him again. Too proud to turn around again, Paula sat there, wounded pride and all.

"I'm so stupid", she thought. "I guess Katie is a regular now."

With hymns beginning already, Tommy had time only to lean forward and whisper in Paula's ear, "Please wait after church. I want to talk with you".

Tommy sat behind Paula just watching her. "She is so beautiful", he thought, and the urge to lean forward and touch her was almost more than he could resist.

Paula sat there, eyes fixed straight ahead, as if staring into space. She rehearsed a hundred times the image her mind had captured of Tommy being seated behind her with Katie beside him.

I hope my sermon did someone some good, but I know it was totally lost on Paula and Tommy. Barely waiting until "amen", Tommy was on his feet and reaching for Paula's shoulder. Turning around, her tortured eyes met his.

"Paula, there's someone I want you to meet," Tommy said. Taking Katie by the hand, he presented her to Paula. "This is my sister, Mary Katherine."

"THIS IS MY SISTER, Mary Katherine..." replayed in slow motion in Paula's mind. A blank look accompanied by "Oh, yes", as she took a deep breath. "Yes, I'm very glad to meet you. Tommy has mentioned you fondly many times. You're very pretty."

"Well, he has certainly told me lots about you," Mary Katherine volunteered as she smiled.

"Paula, may I drive you home?" Tommy asked. Reaching for his hand she replied, "Yes, Tommy. I'd like that." On the way home Paula could hardly contain her excitement. "His sister," she thought.

"Paula, let's drive over to Blue Ridge. We can get something to eat and we'll have time to talk."

"Okay, Tommy. I'll change clothes and tell Mom and Dad where we're going".

As they left Paula's home, Tommy said, "At last we can talk, face to face. Paula, I missed you so much at Christmas."

"I know, I know", she said, "me, too."

Words failed Tommy as his soul begged for freedom to express what was pent up inside him. Unable to find the right words, he pulled into a small roadside picnic area. He brought the pickup to a sudden stop. Then, without a word, he gently pulled Paula close to him and passionately kissed her.

"Oh, Tommy," she sighed. "We have so much to talk about."

Holding hands, they drove slowly toward Blue Ridge. In no time at all, they were at <u>Charlie's Quick Stop</u>. That same corner booth where they had been before, awaited them. That early January day they saw no people; they smelled no food. Time stood still as they exchanged smiles of adoration, laughing like children at play.

"Paula, you left the Sunday morning before Christmas so quickly; and you had that guy with you. Then you spent Christmas with his family; I didn't understand."

"Oh, Tommy, if I had only known". Then she explained about seeing him with *that girl* and seeing them the second time in this very diner. "There was the teddy bear, the ring, and all that..."

Paula cried as Tommy again explained to her that "that girl" was Katie, his little sister.

"I know, I know", she said.

"And the teddy bear and ring were for you. I was so excited about getting them for you that I had to share my excitement with Katie. She had just gotten home for Christmas break. Oh, Paula, I was so lonely when you left... and I didn't understand".

"When I saw you and Katie together, I was so hurt that I wanted to run. Mark had asked me to spend Christmas with his family. I had not decided for sure about it but when I saw you and Katie together in church, I couldn't wait to leave. I had to escape."

Tommy held both her hands across the table and with piercing blue eyes said, "Paula, I'm in love with you. I've loved you from the first day I met you. I think I realized it the day we sat right here and talked so long. I didn't want to let you know how much I cared because it was too sudden and I didn't want to scare you away".

"Tommy, I have loved you just as long. The time we spent here, the time on the Christmas tree hunt..."

"You wouldn't sit beside me on the sleigh", he remembered.

"Oh, Tommy, I cared so much for you, and so suddenly, that it scared me. I felt that I needed to back off a little, but I never stopped caring. It wouldn't go away."

The remainder of that day and every day thereafter, Tommy and Paula made time for each other. Even though she would go back to college after the New Year, they would not be separated in love or in spirit.

CHAPTER 14

M onday morning was here again really fast. Sunday had gone well at church. Many people had reflected on the past year and committed themselves to greater service for God in the coming year. This afternoon will be my second session with the Anderson boys. I had heard of no trouble over the weekend. Millie had been in church Sunday morning. Yes, things had gone well.

Ben and Bart were punctual arriving at 4:55 p.m. I had each one recite John 1:11-12 and John 3:16-17. We then reviewed the whole third chapter before moving on to chapters 4 and 5. I zeroed in on John 4:14 where it reads: "*...but whosoever drinketh of the water that I shall give him shall never thirst; but the water that I shall give him shall be in him a well of water springing up into everylasting life.*" This is your memory verse for Wednesday, New Years Eve.

Again the boys were very punctual on Wednesday. They recited their memory verses and intelligently discussed the written word. I realized that is exactly what it was to them, only the written word, for it had not penetrated their hearts where it could impart new life. At any rate, I was proud of their knowledge of the scriptures even though it was only head knowledge.

As evening turned into night, I put the finishing touches on a devotional I had prepared for the New Years Watch Night service. I was astonished as a wave of inspiration came over me. I'll use the same scripture I gave to the boys - John 4:14. "*But whosoever drinketh of the water...*" I completely disregarded the other devotional and started developing a new one around this scripture.

About 7:30 the phone rang. It was Ma Mac. She apologized for not being able to come to the Watch Night service but said Aaron's arthritis was acting up and he couldn't drive. She added that even with her spectacles she couldn't see to drive at night. I asked her if they could come if someone gave them a ride. "Oh yes, Pastor, we'd love to come".

"Okay, Ma Mac. Be ready and someone will be there to pick you up, I promise". I knew I couldn't go. The next best choice was Tommy. I knew he and Paula would help so I phoned him.

"Sure, Pastor", was his reply. Paula and I will be glad to pick them up. I then put the finishing touches on the devotional and closed my bible.

We had a wonderful service that New Year's Eve night. I opened the service for personal testimonies as we all looked back on the past year. Different ones stood to tell of a special blessing or experience. Harry Chance spoke up first.

"Pastor, I have never experienced as much joy as I did when we went caroling. Why, I couldn't carry a tune in a bucket but when I was mixed in with everybody else, it didn't sound so bad." His voice broke as he lowered his head. Clearing his throat, he continued. "It was pure joy to help others; and the children, oh, the children." He swallowed, trying to talk in spite of the lump in his throat. He began again slowly. "I grew up very poor. Christmas was always very special but we never had many toys or treats. When I saw the little faces looking up, smiling as we gave them candy and toys, it broke my heart. I never realized we had such needs here in Stone Gap. God help me, where have I been?" These simple words, born out of such heartfelt conviction, were so profound that there was dead silence.

While folks were still clinging to Harry's words, John Mason stood. "Pastor, I'd like to stand as a witness to God's grace, love, and mercy. As most of you know, we're relatively new here in Stone Gap. I want to share that God, this past year, brought my wife Sarah through cancer with a clean bill of health and without surgery." He hesitated, lips trembling. In a breaking voice, he continued. "It was quite an ordeal but God was faithful. Shortly after transferring here, a tree, a very big tree, fell across my jeep. I hit my head on the steering wheel and was knocked unconscious but sustained no other injuries. God spared my life. Naturally, there was the uncertainty of "pulling up roots" and coming to a new location. Well, let me tell you, we like it just fine. This is home now." Cheers broke out and Tommy and Paula beamed. I've never seen a couple more in love.

Aaron and Daisy stood up. Aaron began, "All these years, all the children that have grown up and now have children of their own…all these years we have had the priviledge to witness life in these mountains with you good people. We love you all so much." He paused, rubbed his chin, and chuckled. "Why, this old beard is older than most of you, so you can take it from an old man, God is faithful". Then he seemed to gather steam as he said, "He was faithful to Abraham; He was faithful to Moses; He was faithful to David; He was faithful to Daniel and the three Hebrew children; He was Faithful to Paul. He brought us through the great depression; He brought us through the war; He brought us through the death of our children; He healed our bodies; He saved our souls…" Daisy was praising God but not alone. The entire congregation was on its feet, praising God with uplifted hands.

Helen and I lay in bed that night reviewing the service and, indeed, the whole time we had been in Stone Gap. As peaceful slumber overtook us, Helen summed it up beautifully with, "Oh peaceful and majestic night. I wonder what this New Year will bring."

CHAPTER 15

I never did like jail. I have been blessed when visiting there, but I never liked going there. No, I have never liked jail! Did I say that? Well, here I am this January 2nd in jail. No, not just visiting…I'm in jail! You may remember my casually mentioning those Anderson boys. Well, they are a rowdy pair. I did mention that, too? "Hell-raisers" no less!

Ben and Bart were doing really well with their punctuality, manners, and bible study. We had completed three sessions of therapy. I guess the overwhelming urge to scrap got the better of them on New Year's Eve night. It seems that the city police over in Blue Ridge arrested two twenty year old guys; each was wearing only a diaper pinned on with large blue safety pins, a pacifier tied around his neck, drunk, and painted across his chest was "It's a Boy!"

Under the prevailing circumstances, I was the first one to be called since I had them remanded into my custody and had taken full responsibility for their actions. The police did not throw me in jail, but through the proper authorities, I requested to be locked up and let the boys go free.

"Your Honor", I told the Judge, "I'm not just playing a game with the law. I'm in a battle to change lives. These boys have got to learn."

"I understand what you're trying to do, Reverend, but I do this reluctantly", he said. He then told the police chief to let the Anderson boys go and to lock me up.

The food was surprisingly good. I couldn't say the same, however, for the atmosphere or décor. I used my one phone call to tell Helen where I was. "Why don't you ask Paula to spend the night with you, Honey?"

"Okay, Darling", she cried. "I'll be there in the morning to see you."

We have no paper in Stone Gap. We don't need one! "The preacher's in jail!...The preacher's in jail..." It rang across our community almost like the game Red Rover..."Red Rover, Red Rover, send the jailbird right over!" The word got around to every nook and cranny, every Gramp and Granny, every beauty shop, garden shop, barber shop, grocery store, any place where verbal communication could travel.

Helen came; Helen cried; Helen laughed; and laughed and cried. "You crazy man, you crazy wonderful man." Holding my hands through the bars, she said the word was out all over Stone Gap. "And the reason you're here is out, too."

About that time, Paula and Tommy came in. "Pastor, there is a quiet and eerie calm hanging over the community", Tommy said. "I've never seen anything like it. I think you're moving mountains". Paula nodded in agreement. After about an hour, I told Helen to leave my bible and to go back home. I assured her I would be all right.

"I'll stay another night with her, Pastor," Paula volunteered.

"Crazy Man... I love you", Helen said as they left.

The first night I had a private suite. Due to the pressing need for additional accommodations, the second night it became a semi-private, then a semi-semi private suite. One white, one black, and one Hispanic. Thank heavens everyone could speak English. We hit it off really well immediately with many things in common - we were all men, we all liked to eat...did I say many things in common? I forgot what the other things were!

I decided to use this time of leisure to good advantage. Our suite joined bar-to-bar with many other suites, and with all filled to capacity, I'd say we had around a dozen in attendance; smelly, cursing, spitting, swearing, unshaven, drunk. With such a captive audience, I decided to have church. I opened the service with *Jesus Loves Me This I know for the bible tells me so.* It got really quiet and then the second time around, a few others joined in. One guy in a corner didn't quite understand what was going on and requested that we sing Ninety-Nine Bottles of Beer on the Wall. I didn't feel that this would be appropriate for the occasion so he deferred to Michael Rowed the Boat Ashore. As we sang Amazing Grace, the spitting, cursing, and swearing ceased. Guys began to sober up. I couldn't get away from the scripture, John 4:14, *But whosoever drinketh of the water that I shall give him shall never thirst.* My soul convulsed within me as the inspiration of scripture seemed to flow from me. The admonition to walk the path of right, to turn from any form of evil spilled over the boundaries of race, color, or station in life for we were all drenched in the spirit of God as it decended on us like a cloud.

"But the water that I shall give him shall be in him a well of water springing up into everlasting life". Then crying and moaning erupted all over as calloused men began to call on God and repent. No one needed to tell them how…they just repented. It was such a stirring sight that the next morning , the Judge came to the jail. He had been made aware of the situation early in the morning and came to see for himself.

"Reverend", he said sternly, "are you responsible for this?"

"No, Your Honor, Jesus did it."

The Judge was dumbfounded in so much that he ordered that I be released.

"Your Honor, I have to stay", I said. He smiled understandingly and said, "Lock him back up, Bob".

I never did like jail. When those cold steel bars clanked shut behind me, I liked it even less. I thought, "My God, a soul imprisoned by sin has no freedom of movement, no freedom to live, no freedom to express. Christ Jesus is the key to open that prison. Please give me wisdom to use that key."

And the evening and the morning were the third day. Ten o'clock a.m. brought visitors. "Reverend, I could get something done at the Court House if I weren't having to come down here to see you so much. Good thing the jail is close by!"

"Good morning, Your Honor", I said.

"Reverend, you have two guys who want to see you. Come in,

Ben and Bart", the Judge said. "These guys want to go to jail and send you home. He turned his head away, paused and cleared his throat.

"But, Your Honor", I argued. "I agreed to take their place".

"Please, Pastor", the boys begged, "please go home. Let us take our medicine." They continued pleading with me in apologetic tones. "Please, go home."

"You are free to go, Reverend", said the Judge.

"I know, Your Honor, but may I please stay with these guys?" I requested. He was very understanding about my concern for Ben and Bart. He knew I was making progress with them. Although there were empty cells now, the Judge told the jailer to put us all in the same cell.

Helen came, Helen cried. Helen almost giggled trying to hide a grin for she could see the humiliation on the boys' faces.

"Guys, this is my wife, Helen. Honey, this is Ben and this is Bart".

"Very pleased to meet you, Mrs. Slater".

"I met your Mom last week", Helen said. "She's a very nice lady".

"Yes Ma'am, she said you and Pastor Slater stopped by", Ben responded.

I peered through the bars and found complete understanding in Helen's eyes. She whispered that Paula was outside waiting for her. "Any idea when..?" she started.

"Shh", I jestured. "Maybe soon".

By the time that Helen had departed, it was almost noon and time for lunch. Lunch was fair but seemed to bear a marked resemblance to lunch yesterday. The décor was sort of settling in on me now. At first it was hard to get used to gray-on-gray. Kinda like looking at the side of a battleship up close!

"Well, guys, looks like we've got this resort all to ourselves. Let's have the blessing."

The boys didn't sit down to lunch immediately. They seemed to take turns pacing back and forth staring through the bars like a tiger at the circus. All the attributes were there except the roar. Eventually, they seemed to settle down. With nothing for them to do but think, I decided to let them do just that - think. Not wanting to disturb their thought processes, I lay back on the bunk and took a nap. Although I was awakened by low conversation, I didn't let them know.

"Man, we're a sorry lot. Look at us. Mom's hurt and everybody knows about us. We've even gotten the Preacher locked up. If I ever get out of this mess, I'm straightening up", said Bart.

"Praise God", I whispered to myself.

They continued in almost unintelligible whispers reminiscing about childhood and doing things with Dad. "Remember how he used to shine our shoes for Sunday School and always made sure we had a neat haircut?"

" Yeah, and how we fished in the creek? And how about that night we all camped on the sandbar and got roasted marshmellows in our hair? I thought the ants would eat us up." They snickered like ten year olds again.

"Come and get it", shattered the quiet. "Time to eat" was announced as the officer brought in three Styrofoam boxes with our supper.

"Just like the army", I said. "Three hots and a cot!"

The boys just looked at each other and then sat down to eat. Looking very much like leftovers from lunch, I figured we were eating from someone's buffet which had been prepared at ten o'clock. and had gone through the aging process forthwith!

The more I looked at those gray walls, the smaller the cell became. I lay back on the bunk after supper and escaped into my thought world. I figured it was going to be a bad night for the boys, and right now, I wanted them to 'marinate' a little longer in this quagmire of stinch they had brought themselves to.

I wonder if Ole Silas and Dog ate those goodies I took to them after Christmas... I wonder how long it will be before Tommy asks Paula to marry him... How can the church reach out and help more people...? I wonder if Ole Silas' stream has any trout in it. I felt that my creative mind had revolted. I didn't want to think. Man, this place is such a bore...not even a paper to read! No frills hotel! See if I come back!! I'll take my business somewhere else, I jested mentally.

I knew that if, in all my aged wisdom, this place was getting to me, it must surely be torture to these young bucks, these untamed spirits, the scourge of the county. Evening turned to night. Things were fairly quiet until around 10 o'clock when two drunks were brought in.

"Separate these two", the Officer said to the jailer. "They like to fight".

I didn't say anything. I just watched Ben and Bart out of the corner of my eye. The drunks were loud and profane. The jailer locked them in separate cells before uncuffing them. When the cuffs came off, each one immediately lunged for the other through the bars. "You sorry _ _ _ _ ! And _! Not a pretty sight, but needful I think. This raping of the eardrums by such degradation of the English language continued till around midnight when they finally succumbed to exhaustion and sleep. Snoring never sounded so good!

I wasn't sleepy and the boys were in a talkative mood. "Preacher, why are you here? You could be home with your wife. You don't deserve this".

"Guys, Christ took our place on the cross. He didn't deserve that. He took our penalty. He paid the price of our freedom. I'm not going to preach. You guys know the bible better than most. I just wanted to go through this with you."

They wouldn't have been any quieter or less speechless if I had hit them in the head with a 2 x 4. "You have been given a 'Get-Out-of-Hell-Free' card. What you do with it is up to you."

And the evening and the morning were the fourth day. And very early in the morning, the Judge came to the 'sepulchure' where we were entombed.

"Now look here, Reverend, you've got to leave", he said emphatically. "It seems that somebody knew somebody's uncle, who knew someone in Atlanta. Anyway, the Atlanta newspapers have picked up the story and reporters have been flooding the county switchboard with calls all night. I agreed to a short interview around noon, but I'd rather not have you here for pictures, if you understand what I mean. I can see the headlines now; "LOCAL JUDGE JAILS INNOCENT MINISTER".

"I see your point, Your Honor. What's your suggestion?"

"Take these, these...anyway, please go home and take them with you".

By the time His Honor got to "and take these", Ben and Bart had their jackets and were ready to vacate the premises. "Guys, where's your car?" I asked. We felt free as birds out of a cage, as indeed, we were.

I called "shotgun" as Ben drove and Bart got into the back seat. "You still have license?" I teased.

"Yes, sir", Ben smiled.

The winding road and rolling panarama were especially beautiful as we breathed in the fresh air. As we pulled into my driveway, I thanked them for the ride and left them with these words of wisdom; "a shower surely will feel good!"

CHAPTER 16

My time in jail had taken up most of the week. Sunday was upon me again. I had some scattered ideas for a sermon but nothing that really inspired me. My thoughts took me to Dahlonega and the gold mines. Then the sermon title came to me, "What Things Have Worth".

A cold blustery day might have given reason to others to stay home, but our congregation had become fused into a family of belivers. When one suffered, we all suffered; when one rejoiced, we all rejoiced. With the exception of some who were sick, most of the regulars were there. As I looked over the congregation this morning, I noticed that Millie Anderson had taken her seat on the third row. She was greeted with such enthusiasm that she disappeared from sight as the people hovered around her. We were about ready to start singing when *what to my wondering eyes did appear but a noisy red Ford and two cavaliers.* Dressed like lawyers in three piece suits and spit- shined shoes, Ben and Bart marched right into church, up to the third row and sat on each side of Millie. Her joy radiated so much and she was so excited, I thought she was going to have a coronary right there. As we sang, I rejoiced greatly at seeing them.

I began my sermon, " <u>What Things Have Worth?</u>" I read from I Peter 1:7, "*...that the trial of your faith, being much more precious than of gold that perisheth, thought it be tried with fire, might be found unto praise and honor and glory at the appearing of Jesus Christ.* Ask most people what is valuable and they will say, gold.

While this is very true, many do not know why gold is valuable and why it is sought after by so many. To begin with, gold is rare. Because it is rare, it continues to hold its value from ancient times until now. Gold is one of the most ductile metals. It is the most malleable metal. It is pretty and will not tarnish, making it an excellent choice for jewelry. It is an excellent conductor of electricity. Gold has a variety of uses including dentistry, medicine, and electronics. The purer gold becomes, the more valuable it is. Do you know what purifies gold? Fire purifies gold. The hotter the fire, the purer it becomes." I continued, "that's why the refining of gold is compared to our walk with Christ. Our faith will be tried also, but through these firey trials, it will be purified. Instead of passing away, our faith will become praise and honor to God. So I ask you this question: What in your life has worth? Are there precious things in your life that are contaminated with impurities? God's Holy Spirit can burn out the impurities and make your life more precious, more rare, and more productive. I open the altar to everyone who desires to partake in this process."

As everyone stood, two good-looking young men on the third row boldly came forward and knelt. Though they had not seen the inside of the church in years, the pathway to the cross was familiar as they found their way home, a longing, I believe, that is inherent in everyone. We only have to ask Jesus to help us find the way.

Tuesday afternoon found me in my study thinking about the coming spring and what I might want to plant in my garden. Tomatoes were first on my list. Will I plant Big Boys, Better Boys, or just stick to Rudgers, which have always been a favorite? I was lost in thought when a middle-aged woman rushed in and exclaimed, "Preacher, come quickly. Ms. Goss just died and there is nobody to call. The children are just frantic!"

I phoned Helen and asked her to meet me at the Goss residence. "Mrs. Chastain, will you notify the ladies?" I found my way through many of the same streets we had driven while caroling and, in fact, found that the Goss home was one of the homes we had visited.

Alice Goss was a single mom with two children and no near relatives. Sammy and Alicia were ages ten and eight. Alice was a very frail lady, maybe thirty years old. She had become ill yesterday with flu-like symptoms and passed away suddenly this afternoon. When I arrived at the house, the children were crying and in a state of shock. Only two neighbor ladies were there to await the funeral director. I was not prepared for what was taking place so suddenly. I was relieved when Helen arrived to lend support. As she began to console the children, I quietly began to question the neighbor ladies about next of kin, friends, or anyone else close to the family. As far as I could determine, Alice Goss and her two children were pretty much alone. I knew this was going to be tough on the children and I wasn't eager to look into their questioning, innocent eyes and tell them how much God loves them. Kinda had a hollow sound, I thought. What these kids needed wasn't so much the spiritual right now. They needed practical, down-to-earth, heartfelt love.

"Wait a second, Old Man. I've got to wipe my spectacles." What a relief, I thought. Like a breath of fresh air, Aaron and Daisy walked in and love entered the room. We exchanged only nods as they knelt down on eye-level with the kids and hugged them. Helen instinctively stepped aside and we watched as the children responded to Aaron and Daisy's expression of love. Mrs. Chastain had done well for Aaron and Daisy were some of the first ones she had contacted.

Funerals are not easy at best. This was a difficult situation for me. I didn't know Alice Goss and, more importantly, I didn't know her standing with the Lord. There was, however, a family bible on the coffee table so I relied on it for much information. It recorded birthdays and deaths of her mother and father. No siblings were there, no record of marriage; not much to go on but a certificate of baptism in a Primitive Baptist church when Alice was ten years old, location not listed. This was one consolation. I knew that if she were baptized as a Primitive Baptist, that she had given her life to Jesus as a child. I believe when people die that they go to heaven or to hell; there is no in-between! So as I was thinking about Alice's funeral, I was wondering what I could say that would be appropriate, both comforting and truthful.

During the funeral I leaned heavily on grace and mercy as a general theme, giving praise to a courageous mother who, as a single parent, raised her children with loving care. Aaron and

Daisy, who had kept the children with them since the death, sat with them during the service and later at the cemetery.

I had been thinking ahead to the question, "where will Sammy and Alicia go now". As I said the last amen over the grave, Aaron stroked his beard and asked me quietly, "Pastor, where will the kids go?"

"I don't know yet, Pa Mac", I responded.

"Well, Pastor, Daisy and I have been cogitating about this. We've got plenty of space and live close to the road for the school bus". He continued, "why couldn't they stay with us for a while?" His eyes were wet with tears as his lips trembled under his gray beard. "Pastor, you think you could arrange it?" He pleaded. "Daisy would be so happy".

I can't say that I hadn't thought about it before, because I had. It seemed to be a really logical thing to do at the time, at least for the short term. I knew there was enough love in their home to go around. I told Aaron to take the kids home with them for now and that I would deal with the Department of Family and Childrens Services about it.

Upon investigation by the agent for DFACS, Aaron and Daisy were awarded temporary custody of the children. For now, that was all that was needed to help heal the hurts of two small children and rescue them from a sea of uncertainty. Enthusiasm reigned to such a degree at the McHenry house that Aaron and Little Sammy designed a shingle to hang under the mailbox which read:

THE McHENRYs

Aaron
Daisy
Sammy
Alicia

CHAPTER 17

"Honey, there's an old bag on the front porch", Helen said. "Well, ask her to leave," I teased. "You know I don't want old bags hanging around here. People might talk."

"Silly Man", she said, as I went to the porch.

Opening the bag I saw only a scribbled note, "Goss kids", and $100 in small bills. "What? Who?" Then it dawned on me. The whole meaning became clear. This was the canvas bag I had used to take goodies to Ole Silas after Christmas. He somehow knew it was from me and where to find me. Now he was offering a part of himself to someone else and entrusting me as executor of his offering. I saw in this gesture acceptance, trust, and caring, not at all the "wild man of the mountains" some local myths portrayed.

I felt it was time for a haircut. Finding out about Ole Silas would be my quest for today.

Ting-a-ling

"Hello, Pastor".

"Hi, Ned. Hi, Fellows".

Four ole-timers, two twelve or thirteen year olds, Ned and I… that ought to be enough input about Ole Silas, I thought.

"Say, Ned. What's the word on an old hermit who lives around here?" I broke in.

"Pastor, about all I know is that some old man lives alone up in the hills. They say he's a big man and always has his dog with him."

"Yeah," another spoke up, "a big man, about six feet six. Yeah, a big man."

One of the boys spoke up and said, "I always heard that he eats chickens raw after he bites off their heads."

The other boy said he heard that someone saw Silas on a moonlight night walking on all fours through the cemetery.

"How old is he?" I asked. The boys agreed that he must be about a hundred and twenty five years old.

"Raw chicken must be pretty healthy," I mused.

One of the older men volunteered, "He never has bothered anybody or anything, as far as I know. He just lives to himself. I've heard that he went into seclusion after his wife died in childbirth."

That coincided, pretty much, with what Tommy had told me. Well, I had found out what I wanted to know and, after my turn in the chair, I left with the intent of enlarging my channel of communication with Ole Silas.

A stop at Harry Chance's general store should fill in the gaps in my overall knowledge of Ole Silas. I browsed the store drinking a coke, until Harry was not busy with customers. "Harry, if it wouldn't be breaking a confidence, tell me what you know about Ole Silas."

"Okay, Pastor. What do you want to know?"

"Where did he come from? Does he have family? How does he live? What does he look like?"

Harry said, "I don't know where he came from, or if he has any family. I guess he's always been here. He comes in a couple of times a month and buys mostly staples, you know, flour, sugar, coffee, and beans. He always pays cash and never asks for credit. Oh, yes, he buys kerosene on a regular basis and a few .22 bullets and shotgun shells. As to what he looks like, I don't really know, except he's big, really big; tall, and has a deep raspy voice."

"What about his face?" I asked.

"Don't really know, Pastor. Never have seen it completely. He has blue eyes, I remember that."

"Why have you never seen his face?"

"Well, Silas always wears an old military-looking pile cap pulled down over his ears and buttoned under his chin. Really strange. Another thing, Pastor, he has a way with animals. Dogs won't even bark at him."

"Harry, where does his money come from?"

"I know he does some trapping, but I don't know what else he does."

"Thanks, Harry, you've been a big help."

One thing I knew for sure, Ole Silas didn't have a mailbox. I thought the next logical step would be to check with the post office to see if he had a post office box. The Post Mistress, Mrs. Pendley, was really skeptical and reluctant to help at first, but when I showed her my credentials and explained the nature of my mission, she agreed to help.

"Bingo, there it is", she said. "S. J. Vinson. Post Office Box 0045. That's one of the oldest boxes. He's had it for a long time. I never have seen him but five or six times. He must come for his mail in the evening when the window is already closed".

"Does he get much mail?" I ventured.

"Not much, mostly just a government check."

Although she was very cooperative, I didn't want to be too invasive. I only wanted to arm myself with information that would enable me to reach Silas. I felt the unrelenting urge to pursue and unravel the mystery Silas had presented to me. I invited Mrs. Pendley to church and thanked her.

I told Helen everything I had learned. I knew that my newfound knowledge would be safe with her and would also help her realize my passion in this matter. Contact with Ole Silas could only be made by patience and planning. If he had gone into seclusion so long ago to withdraw from the human race, bringing him back, if indeed I could at all, would be a very arduous task. I therefore planned a one-man fishing expedition up the valley in hopes of further facilitating my goal of reaching him.

One rod, one small tackle box with an assortment of flys, one creel, one canteen, one can of Vienna sausage and some saltines, now I was ready to go. As usual, I told Helen where I would be and about what time to expect me back. "If I'm not back on time, call Tommy."

I felt more confident this time having been up the valley one time before. There was no snow and no tracks to follow. I slowly and quietly made my way to a point maybe half a mile from where I had seen the tracks the last time I was here — any further and the trout stream became really narrow. The day was brisk but sunny and the wind was calm. I found a likely looking pool and began casting. "Beautiful stream, simply beautiful", I thought. The angle of the winter sun on the shimmering water sparkled with the brilliance of a thousand diamonds. The misted rocks and smooth stones gleamed with a myriad of colors. This was worth the trip if there were no fish at all.

This was not the case, however, for suddenly, jerk, jerk,... "Gotcha!" I said to myself, "Man, a 14 inch rainbow." I cast again and caught another one but it was not a keeper. I backed away from the pool in an effort not to spook the fish. "I'll give it a few minutes to settle down", I said. I then remembered what I had heard one time, "It's all right to talk to yourself, but when you start answering yourself, you've really got a problem"!

I took a drink from my canteen, put it back in my canteen belt, and laid it on the ground. Feeling refreshed, I moved slowly to the edge of the pool and cast again. Wham! Water swirling! Fish flouncing! "A whopper...man, what a fish! Rod tip up! Don't let him off! Okay! A 15 inch brown trout."

That worked pretty well, so I backed off again. I repeated this two or three more times with varying degrees of success. I reached around for my canteen but when I couldn't find it, I looked behind me. I stood up, took a few steps, but it was not to be seen. Feeling not a little confused, I glanced around toward the tree line. There among the trees, I caught a glimpse of movement. Some type of animal but I couldn't make it out. I decided to continue fishing but to keep an eye on the woods also. The fishing was not quite the same after that. I knew "it" was watching me, whatever "it" was. "There must be something I need to do at home", I reasoned, and I left; I just left! "Bear, panther, wolf, who knows?"

I let my mind run away until I realized I was hiking at a pretty good pace and was out of breath. Slowing down now and regaining some of my composure, I came to a bend in the trail. "What in the world? How?" There was my canteen and canteen belt hanging from a bush over the trail. It had been strategically placed there so I couldn't miss it. Then it dawned on me what had happened. Dog had stolen my canteen and Ole Silas had backtracked my trail and returned it, never heard nor seen. I knew he was there, somewhere. "Thank you", I shouted, and walked on, confident that I had made contact a second time with this man of mystery.

CHAPTER 18

Since I couldn't find a suitable reason to put it off, I made my way to the clinic for my annual checkup. When I was in the army, I had many, many shots. It didn't bother me at all; but at some point, things changed. Now, if I watch anyone getting a shot, I start feeling woozy in my stomach and start seeing black spots. Now that you've sufficiently gotten the picture, today they needed to draw blood. The "vampire lady", as I teasingly referred to her, had me sit with outstretched arm, tight fist. You know the drill.

"Reverend, you won't have me around much longer to pick on", Nurse Henderson announced.

"Oh," I teased, "going back to Transylvania?"

She cackled. "No Sir, I'm retiring".

"Well, congratulations. When is the big day?"

"The end of March," she said.

"I know you are really looking forward to that." Remembering Paula's graduation, I asked, "Who will replace you? Ouch! Am I bleeding badly where you stuck me with that harpoon?!"

"Oh, I think you'll make it", she quipped.

"You're really very good at what you do, Mrs. Henderson", I said. "We're going to miss you."

"Thank you, Reverend Slater. Oh, to answer your question", she remembered. "I don't know who will take my place. Doctor McPherson will start taking applications soon."

"X-rays look great, heart great. We will call you when we get the lab results, Reverend".

"Thanks, Doctor McPherson."

I went straight home to give Helen the news about the nursing position coming open at the clinic. "Honey, do you have Paula's phone number at school? Why don't you call her right away and see if she's interested in the position?"

"Yes, yes, very much so", Paula replied. "I will come home Friday evening. Will you please pick up an application for me?"

"I'll be glad to", Helen said. "In fact, why don't you and Tommy have dinner with Matthew and me Saturday night and I'll give it to you then. Do you like trout?"

"Sounds good, Mrs. Slater. Just let me clear it with Tommy".

"Hello, Tommy."

"Hey, Paula, how's my girl?"

"Much better now that I hear your voice", she said. "Tommy, I'm coming home Friday evening. I've got a surprise for you when I get there. The Slaters have invited us for dinner Saturday night. Is that okay with you?"

"Yes, that would be fine. Sounds like fun. What time will you get here Friday?"

"Probably around 6 o'clock", she replied.

"Okay if I come over about 7:30? I don't want to rush in on you and your family but I can't wait to see you."

"Me, too," she said. "How 'bout 6:30?"

As Tommy drove up, Paula met him on the porch. "I missed you so much," she sighed.

"I can hardly stand being away from you," he said.

"Not much longer, Tommy", she said. "Let's sit here a while and talk. You know, I graduate in six weeks." Her excitement grew, "and the surprise I have for you is that a nursing position is coming open at the clinic here, right here in Stone Gap. I'm going to apply for it Monday before I go back to school. Mrs. Slater has already gotten the application for me."

"Oh, Paula, that would be wonderful, an answer to prayer".

Saturday evening Tommy and Paula arrived for dinner at 6:30. While Helen was putting the finishing touches on the meal and Paula was pouring tea, Tommy and I relaxed in the den. "Pastor, lots of things have happened since you've been in Stone Gap", Tommy said.

"Yes, Tommy. God has blessed us in so many ways."

Tommy continued reluctantly, "There's something I may want you to do for me; that is, not now, maybe later."

"Tommy, have you asked her yet?"

"Whew!" He sighed. "No, not yet."

"Come to dinner", Helen called.

"We'll talk more later on", I said.

After we had the blessing, Tommy and Paula's eyes locked on each other in a way that reminded me of how it was when Helen and I were first in love. "Majestic" falls pitifully short of describing it.

"Will you have some hush puppies, Tommy?" I said.

"Oh yes, yes sir," he replied.

That seemed to recapture his attention for the time being, I thought.

"Oh, Mrs. Slater, where did you buy these trout", Paula asked. "They're wonderful".

"Oh, I didn't buy them. Matthew caught them"

"Did you really, Pastor?" Tommy questioned.

"Yes, Tommy, I found a nice pool up the valley".

"You mean toward Ole Silas' place?"

"Yes, about two miles up just before the valley narrows", I said. "Confidentially, I have been trying to establish communication with Silas. I'd like to help him if I can."

"It was a wonderful meal, Mrs. Slater. Thank you for inviting us", Tommy said.

"You're very welcome. I'm glad you and Paula could come. You men, go back to the den and talk. Paula and I will clean the kitchen. Besides, we have girl things to talk about", Helen responded.

"Paula, I'm so excited about the possibility of your getting that position at the clinic", Helen said.

"Yes, I am, too. Tommy and I both agree that it would be an answer to prayer."

"Tommy is a very fine young man," Helen said.

"Yes, he's the most gentle, considerate, loving, kind ..." Paula blushed.

"Matthew was all those things, too, and I thought I couldn't live without him", Helen responded.

In the den, I was confiding in Tommy the progress I was making where Ole Silas was concerned.

"You know he eats chickens raw after he bites off their heads, don't you"? He grinned.

"Yes", I responded. "And he's also a hundred and twenty-five years old."

"Yes, at least", Tommy laughed. "I see you have been doing your research! Well, he's got some age on him but he's not a hundred and twenty-five. I'd say, maybe sixty, sixty-five".

"Have you seen him up close?" I asked.

"Yes sir, I almost bumped into him at the general store a couple of years ago".

"I was going in when he was coming out. It was really late in the evening. That's mostly when he travels, I think".

As Helen and Paula came into the den, Helen said, "Okay, kids. Go on now. I know you want some time to be together. You don't have to spend the evening with "old folks".

"Speak for yourself, Woman", I grinned.

Tommy and Paula took the cue and gracefully said, "Goodnight. See you tomorrow morning in church."

"Helen, my Darling, you are wise beyond your years", I said.

After Sunday morning service, Helen and I were standing at the door speaking to everybody as they left. When most of the congregation was gone, Alton and Sue, their children, and Tommy and Paula lingered just talking and having fellowship. I asked Tommy to elaborate more about Ole Silas. When I mentioned his name, the children listened with eagerness. "When you saw him, did he have Dog with him?" I asked.

"Oh, yes," Tommy said. "He never goes anywhere without Dog".

"What does Dog look like?" I asked.

"He's a big, brown German Shepherd with tinges of black down his back. He's big but doesn't appear to be vicious." Tommy dropped Paula's hand, gesturing that the dog was about two feet high at the shoulders.

Yank! Yank! came that familiar tug at my coat that I had come to cherish. "Pastor, I want to meet him," came Robin's little voice.

I knelt down. "You want to meet Ole Silas?"

"Nooo! I want to meet Dog and play with him", she responded.

"Oh, Sweetie, he might bite my "Little Yankee".

"No, he wouldn't. I would be nice to him", she said.

"Well, maybe later", I said.

Robin seemed to be satisfied with that but added, "Now don't forget".

Alton said, "Dad knew Ole Silas in a distant sort of way. He said he knew the girl Ole Silas had married. She was from Mineral Bluff. Molly somebody. Dad went off to the war. After he came home, he said Ole Silas was gone and then about a year later, people reported seeing him once in a while, but mostly in the evenings. Dad went up the valley to see him once but he wanted to be left alone.

"Does he own any land, Alton?" I asked.

"Oh, yes, Pastor. He owns nearly a hundred acres, which borders Chattahoochee National Forest. It's very remote. That's the way he likes it."

The more I heard about Ole Silas, the more intrigued I became with the whole idea of a man becoming a hermit and shutting out the world for almost forty years. He must be so empty, or maybe so hurt that he couldn't find his way back. Whatever the case, I knew he had a need. I decided to try to be his friend.

Two weeks had gone by when Paula was notified that she had been accepted for the position at the clinic. "When can you start?" Dr. McPherson asked.

"I graduate the first week of April. I could start by the 15th", Paula responded.

"That sounds good, Miss Mason. Mrs. Henderson was planning to retire the end of March, but I'm sure she won't mind staying on another two weeks."

Things seem to have become somewhat accelerated with the advent of spring. "In my prophetic mind, I can envision a June wedding", I told Helen.

"Okay, Prophetic Mind", she said. "You've just got a terrific grasp of the obvious!"

"You're right, again" I thought. That was one of the worst kept secrets of the century!

"Has he asked her, yet?" She asked.

"No, Darling, I don't think so".

Paula's graduation was a joyous occasion. Not only did it terminate a rigorous course of study, but it also marked the beginning of a new position in Stone Gap where she would be near her Mom and Dad and her beloved Tommy. Having pre-packed and moved most of her belongings ahead of time, Paula was ready to leave for Stone Gap after the ceremonies. As she and Tommy drove along, he said in a very forthright manner, "Paula, how would you like a hamburger?"

"Well, okay", she said.

"I know this little place with a corner booth. They have the best hamburgers and a good view, too. It's a little out of the way, but it's worth it".

Blue Ridge was "a little" out of the way, about forty miles. The sign read <u>Charlie's Quick Stop and Diner</u>. Tommy pulled in, opened Paula's door, and escorted her as if she had never been there before. He took her directly to the familiar corner booth.

"There is a RESERVED sign on the table", she said.

"I know," he said as he removed the sign. They ordered something; who knows what, maybe a hamburger, or an ice cream cone. They didn't know or care.

"Paula, I wanted to bring you here today because this is our special spot." He reached into his pocket. "I want to give you your graduation present". He handed her a small black velvet box.

"Oh, Tommy!" she gasped. Opening the box she found a beautiful Marquis cut diamond engagement ring.

"Will you marry me, Paula? I love you so much."

"I love you, too, Tommy. Yes! Yes! I'll marry you. That's all I've thought about since the week after Christmas."

Who knows how much time passed? They didn't. Eventually Tommy said, "This has been a perfect day".

She agreed. "Let's go home".

My "prophetic mind" proved to be right on target. After Tommy asked John Mason for permission to marry Paula, Helen and I were the next ones to be notified.

"A June wedding," I remarked to Helen privately. "And who would have thought it."

CHAPTER 19

With the advent of warmer weather and flowering trees, I got a really bad case of fishing fever. With all my fishing gear including Vienna sausage, I headed to my newfound fishing hole. The day was sunny and clear. I told Helen not to be concerned if I were a little later than usual getting back today. Again, I was off on a quest to find out more about Ole Silas.

The trail was easier than before and the two miles didn't seem as far now that I had become familiar with the terrain. I thought to myself, "coming to the cross is not nearly as far as it seemed the first time. The more often we come, the closer it seems."

The narrowing of the valley told me that I was getting near to my mark in the trail where I had first encountered those large tracks in the snow. For a marker, I often leave pieces of small logs in a crossed fashion. This gives me a reference point when in unfamiliar territory. As the forest began to close in around me, I was bathed in the most heavenly fragrances of flowering trees and honeysuckle. This is always one of the joys ushered in by spring.

There was my marker all right. It was different though. Instead of two short logs forming a plus sign, there were three short logs laid across each other perfectly forming a six-pointed star or asterisk. That gave me a weird feeling. I don't mind telling you, that asterisk stayed on my mind. I left my fishing gear at the marker just off the trail. I walked on slowly, looking and listening more than walking. I persistently followed my sense of direction until I saw the clearing just ahead. I felt guilty as I peered from my vantage point in the foliage. Across the clearing, I could see Ole Silas digging in his garden. I looked just to the back of the garden and saw Dog. Dog saw me, too. I knew he was watching me. He never barked, just stared. Savy now to Dog's demeanor, Ole Silas jerked his pile cap from his belt and quickly put it on. I knew I was discovered so I ventured out from my cover and into the clearing. I really didn't know what to do but slowly, very slowly, walked toward them.

I didn't take my eyes off that big dog, and he did not move a muscle. He didn't wag. He just stared. Now as I drew near, I felt dwarfed by this big man. Since it was I who was invading his privacy, I thought I ought to speak first. I really didn't have a good explanation for being here so I began, "Good morning, Silas. I'm …", but before I could tell him my name, he exclaimed in a raspy voice, "By Ned, it's the preacher! Dog, say hello to the preacher." Immediately Dog moved toward me slowly, dropping his head shyly, and wagging his tail.

"Hello, Dog", I responded, as he nuzzled my leg. "Why, he's really very gentle. He wouldn't bite a biscuit", I thought. "Silas, I know I'm on your land without permission but I wanted to meet you."

"Curious, huh?" he asked.

"Yes," I admitted, "curious and concerned. I'll leave if you want me to."

"No, no, you can stay. We don't see too many people. Preacher, I was about to eat some dinner, it's almost noon; you want some?"

"Yes sir, that would be just fine."

Upon entering the very rustic cabin, I was astonished at how clean and orderly he kept it. It was comprised of one large room with hand-hewn table and chairs. A wood-fired cook stove graced one corner. I noticed that it had a "water jacket" to provide hot water. Across the room was a stone fireplace. Its mantle was of heart pine. The floor was well-matched pine with a bearskin rug for décor. The walls had three or four sets of antlers and a few pictures. Off one end of the room was a small bedroom. Over the entrance to the main room was a gun rack.

Ole Silas dipped our food right from the warm pots on the stove.

"Preacher, it's not fancy, just beans and greens, cornbread, and fatback."

"Silas, that sounds good to me. Reminds me of when I was a boy."

His hooded smile showed gray-blue eyes and a weathered face.

"Silas, how long have you lived back here?"

"A long time", he said.

"Have you lived here all your life?" I asked.

"Not yet", he quipped.

His quick-witted reply took me completely by surprise. He smiled at my puzzled expression.

"Silas, this is really tasty. I guess you grow most of your food?"

"I do, by Ned, except for a few things I have to buy at Chance's store."

"Yes, Harry Chance attends our church."

"Yeah, by Ned, he's a good man", Silas proclaimed. "You caught some pretty good fish the other day, Preacher."

"Yes sir, I did", I responded.

"Well, by Ned, you did the right thing not spooking them", he said. "Sometimes you have to just back off and let them settle down."

Although I didn't see him that day, I knew he had been watching me. That's the same day Dog stole my canteen.

"You like to fish, Silas?"

"I do. Like to eat 'um, too, by Ned."

I had heard ole-timers use the expression "by Ned" before, and I realized by now that it was going to be Ole Silas' trademark. It wasn't swearing but was more of an affirmation of his word.

Feeling a little more confident now, I ventured, "there's lots I still need to learn about trout fishing."

"Have some more greens?" He offered.

"Yes, and some more fatback, too."

"By Ned, Preacher, you really know how to eat". He seemed to be pleased to watch me eat. Underneath that pile cap, somewhere behind those gray-blue eyes, I detected a warmth that radiated beyond his rough exterior and raspy voice.

"Silas, I know you're busy with your garden. I don't want to keep you from your work, so I'll be going now. Thanks for dinner. It was really good. Before I go, may I ask you a question?" He didn't answer but just waited for me to ask.

"Why didn't Dog bark at me?"

He chuckled. "Can't! He's mute, by Ned! He can't bark at all!"

"That makes sense", I said.

I realized my expression must have been comical when he burst out with laughter.

"Thanks, Silas. See you."

I hadn't gone ten steps when he called, "Hey, Preacher, if you want to come back, I know where some more good fishing spots are."

Having cracked the door a little, I opened it a little farther. "How 'bout day-after-tomorrow," I ventured. "I don't have anything lined up to do that day."

"That will be fine, by Ned. 'Bout nine?"

I nodded approval and said, "Bye, Dog" as I slowly walked toward the tree line.

The past few hours had been unbelievable. I couldn't wait to tell Helen. I found my way to the marker where I had left my fishing gear. I hadn't told Silas about having it. I wanted nothing to interrupt our line of communication. I didn't care about fishing today but was so much excited about coming back in two days. There was still so much I wanted to ask Silas.

When I told Helen about my adventure, she listened intently with wide-eyed excitement.

"What was his cabin like", she asked. "How did he cook? What kind of furniture did he have?"…all the things you might expect a woman to ask about. "And he invited you to come back and fish? That's wonderful! I can't believe it". Then she added gleefully, "I guess that's not so strange after all, one wild man relating to another!"

"I take no offense. I know you mean it kindly", I remarked.

"Oh?" she smirked, her bright eyes sparkling. I gently swatted her on the rear and hugged her, after which she gave me a big kiss.

The next night I could hardly sleep. I was as excited as a little boy going on a camping trip. It wasn't the fishing so much as the idea of being with Silas again and learning about him. I lay there recalling visually the emerald valley with its fresh spring grass and herbs, the flowering branches, the heavily wooded steeps with their fern- covered floor and over-hanging vines. "By Ned", I thought, "I love it."

I left earlier than usual today so I would be on time. By twenty minutes till nine, I was at my marker and slowed my pace a little, now that I was nearing my destination. As I broke into the clearing, Dog came running toward me wagging his tail. "Good boy", I greeted, "Good boy". I patted his head and stroked his back. He responded by licking my hand and offering his paw to shake hands. Then Ole Silas appeared in the doorway.

"By Ned, Preacher. I think you've found a friend." His voice was still scratchy. The hoarsness had not gone away.

"He's a fine dog", I remarked.

"You ready to fish?" he asked.

"You bet", I replied.

"You're right on time, by Ned," he said. "I like to be on time".

I thought this was a strange attribute for someone who lived in a timeless environment.

"Catch 'um early, cook 'um for dinner, leftovers for supper, I always say."

"Sounds good to me", I nodded.

I followed Silas back to my marker where we veered off the trail through an area of thick cover. Only a few yards beyond, the stream ballooned into a crystal pool maybe fifty feet across where I could see trout swimming among the submerged crevices. Silas beckoned with his hand to crouch down silently and slip up on them. I watched his technique as he cast his first fly. No interest... Second cast, whammo! Rod bent, water splashing, winding, retrieving. "By Ned, Preacher," he whispered, "this is a nice one. Now you give 'um a try. Give it a minute to settle down though."

I nodded. I did give 'um a try, connected, too. Splash!! Splash! Another nice one, another, another, another, until we decided we had enough for our needs. We started slowly for the cabin with our bounty.

"Got some green onions for hush puppies," Silas said. "You like hush puppies?"

"Yes, very much", I said.

We talked about fishing, hunting, nature. Silas was quick-witted and alert. I wanted to know more about him but I knew I'd have to go slowly. "Silas, do you have any family?" I asked.

"Just them", he muttered as he pointed to one long and one short grave. "My sweet wife, Molly. We were married in '38. She died giving birth to our baby girl in the winter of '41...baby died, too. I buried them both near the cabin so I could care for them." His eyes welled up with tears.

"Did you never marry again?"

"Almost. I mean, by Ned, I would have". He began slowly, "Preacher, it's like this. After Molly died in '41, I found myself alone, lonely, and lost. When the Japs attacked Pearl Harbor in December of '41, I figured I might as well go and fight. I joined the army and was stationed at Camp McPherson near Atlanta. After Molly died, I thought I could never find love again. Then I met a beautiful girl named Penny Pope. She worked in a diner in a little place just north of Atlanta. We hit it off right away and talked about getting married. Things happened so fast. I got orders to ship out in two days. We spent my last night together at her place. The next day I was on my way to England. That was June 30, 1942. I never saw her again."

"But didn't you write her?" I asked.

"Oh, yes. We wrote for almost a year. I still have her letters. My letters started coming back in April 1943 marked "NOT AT THIS ADDRESS.""

"I'll fetch a pan so we can clean the fish", Silas said.

He went into the cabin wiping his eyes. I heard him rambling around inside. He called to me on the porch, "Preacher, you are gonna stay and eat, aren't you?"

"You bet! I'm not going to let you have all those fish to your-self. Anyway, I caught the big ones!"

While this was not exactly accurate, I thought it would give him a chuckle. I busied myself talking with Dog while Silas was inside. As the door opened, I turned. I was not prepared for what I saw. Silas stepped out onto the porch. As I grimaced, he instantly wheeled around and ran inside. Upon seeing my face, he realized he had taken off his pile cap while inside and had forgotten to put it back on before he came out.

"I'm sorry, Preacher. I didn't mean to do that," he said.

"Oh, no, Silas. I'm the one who is sorry. Please come out". After a few minutes, Silas came back out with his pile cap in place.

"I guess we had better clean those fish before they spoil," he said.

After a short while I said, "Silas, tell me about your time in the army. Did you get hurt in service?" I asked.

"Yes, Preacher, I did. I was rushing a German position in Belgium when I took a bullet through the side of my neck. That's why I talk this way. Then, by Ned, another German used a flame-thrower on me. I shot him before he could finish the job."

The whole left side of Silas' face was one continuous scar from his cheekbone to the back of his head. Another smaller scar was on his neck just under his jaw also on the left side where the bullet had gone through. His ear was almost completely gone.

"By Ned, I'm not too pretty to look at since then. Only one person besides you has ever seen me without my cap. Aaron McHenry came to see me right after I came home from the hospital in '46. A good man... I thanked him for coming but asked him to let me be alone. He promised he would not tell anyone what he saw. I drank mostly for the next ten years and locked the world out."

"But Silas," I continued, "what about Penny? When you came home in '46, didn't you try to find her?"

"Oh yeah, Preacher," he replied sadly. "I went to where she used to work. They said that my Penny died in April of '43. That's why my letters kept coming back. I visited her grave and put flowers on it."

Silas fired up the stove while I finished filleting the trout.

"Silas, you have done this before, I can tell."

The mouth-watering aroma of trout frying and hush puppies with green onions... Add this to a warm spring day in a heavenly setting and, what can I say?!

"Let's have the blessing, Preacher. Lord, thank you for these victuals. Amen." He continued, "By Ned, I think the trout get better and better. How 'bout some more coffee?"

"Yes, thanks", I said, "good coffee".

After dinner, Silas went into his bedroom and brought back the family bible. "Preacher, I want to show you a picture of Molly". His eyes gleamed as he showed me the yellowed time- stained photo.

"She was pretty, Silas. Is that you with her?" I asked.

"Yes, that's right after we were married."

"But Silas, whose picture is that on the wall?"

"That's Penny," he sighed. "So long ago... I thought I had found happiness again. Then, by Ned, that infernal World War II took everything away."

His last statement echoed in my mind. Yes, World War II not only had taken his Penny away, but his youth, and his stately good looks. I felt heavy with sorrow as he shared his life with me in a way he had not been able to do with anyone in nearly forty years.

"I love children", he said. "I always wanted a son, someone to teach about the outdoors; you know, hunting and fishing..."

"I know," I nodded. I would love to have a son, too. Silas, I know a little girl I think you would love to meet. She is eight years old. Her name is Robin Jones. She had a spinal injury and cannot walk. She said she wanted to meet Dog and play with him."

"Jones? That wouldn't be ole Nathan Jones' grandchild, would it?"

"Yes, it is. Nathan had three children, Alton, Tommy, and Mary Katherine. Robin is Alton's youngest daughter."

"Well, by Ned, I knew ole Nathan Jones. He went off to the war just before me. He came to see me in '46 after I came home but I didn't want anybody around then. Good family, good folks."

"Silas, this little girl means the world to me. Do you think that she could see Dog sometime? You don't have to decide now. You can think about it."

Silas seemed reluctant about the idea but didn't downright refuse. I took this as a positive sign. I never approached Silas from a religious standpoint. If my thimble-full of wisdom was telling me anything, it was saying that Silas was carrying a lot of hurt and was probably bitter toward God. This degree of deep hurt and bitterness can incapsulate a soul in a shell so thick that it can only be peeled away one layer at the time. I felt like I had reached his limit for today.

"Silas, it's getting late. I'd better go", I said.

He followed me to the porch where Dog was waiting for him.

As I was going down the steps, I turned to him. "Silas, my name is Matthew. Please call me Matthew."

"Okay, Preacher", he smiled.

I didn't push Silas, but Robin had asked to see Dog and I thought this would give Silas something to think about. While the door was opening, I might be able to use this to draw him out. "Oh, how great the darkness when one's mind is darkened". Silas had the light shut off very suddenly, very painfully, and the darkness forbade the light for forty years. Now that the light was beginning to shine again, I knew its continuance would eventually dispel every shadow in every corner of his tormented soul.

CHAPTER 20

R ebecca Ellis started attending our church sometime between Thanksgiving and Christmas. Helen and I had spoken to her many times but her responses always seemed distant and noncommittal. A shy girl, she always came alone and never stayed to talk very much with anyone. She seemed always in a hurry to leave. Although she was neat in appearance, it was obvious that she was from a poverty situation. Helen found out that she was a senior in high school.

On this particular Sunday morning, I noticed Rebecca crying. I sent a note to Helen about her. Helen looked at the note, then at me, and nodded in understanding. After the benediction, Helen made her way sensitively to Rebecca who, by now, was nearing the door.

"Rebecca, we're so glad you came this morning".

At this display of concern, Rebecca wheeled around and hugged Helen. She clung to her for a few moments sobbing. "Thanks, Mrs. Slater, I needed that."

On Thursday morning our phone rang. It was Nurse Henderson at the clinic.

"Mrs. Slater, Rebecca Ellis is here and asking for you. Can you come to the clinic?"

Helen responded immediately, "Yes, Mrs. Henderson, I'll be there in a few minutes. Is Rebecca all right?"

"Yes, she is okay but upset."

Helen left right away. The urgency in Mrs. Henderson's voice told her that everything was not well with Rebecca. Arriving at the clinic, Helen found her sitting in the waiting area alone, crying and shivering as if cold, although the room was comfortably warm. When Rebecca saw Helen she stared up at her in a trance-like manner. Her eyes were red, hair disheveled, cheeks streaked with tears.

"Honey, I came as fast as I could", Helen said. Reaching down to Rebecca who was still seated, she hugged her. After a moment of silent concern, Helen sat down and, holding Rebecca's hands gently asked "Rebecca, do you want to talk about it?"

They just sat there speechlessly. Rebecca didn't look up. After a few more minutes of silence, Helen asked, "would you like some coffee?" Rebecca nodded and Helen went to the coffee machine. When she returned, Helen said, "it's a cold day, maybe this will help." Rebecca's shivering subsided as she became more composed. Eventually she looked at Helen and started crying as she spoke, "Mrs Slater, I have a big problem. I'm pregnant. I thought I might be before Christmas. I considered having an abortion, but when I heard Pastor Slater speaking about "A Child at Christmas", I knew that abortion was out of the question. I live with my grandparents. They are poor but very good people. They do the best they can for me. I just don't know how I'm going to tell them. I've had a hard time hiding my morning sickness from them. Mrs Slater, this is a small community. Everyone will know. What can I do?" she bawled.

"Rebecca, where do you live?"

When Rebecca described where she lived, Helen realized that we had stopped there the night the church had gone caroling. "Didn't the carolers stop at your house Christmas Eve?"

"Yes, Ma'am."

"I met your grandmother that night," Helen remembered. "Your grandfather smoked a pipe."

"Yes, Ma'am," Rebecca said as she regained control.

"Rebecca, would you like for me to go with you to talk with your grandmother?"

"Would you please, Mrs. Slater?" Rebecca responded.

"Rebecca, you are seventeen and have made a serious mistake, but through Christ Jesus you can put mistakes behind you and live a happy life."

"I know, Mrs. Slater. I've asked Jesus into my heart but I just don't know how to deal with my problem."

"Well, Rebecca, you've taken the first step by coming to Jesus. Now let's see what we can do about everything else."

Rebecca was relieved to find Helen's support. Helen had a prayer with her and asked God's blessing on her life, her child, and upon the pending situation. With more people coming into the waiting room now, Helen suggested that she and Rebecca go to the car where they could talk in private. Upon reaching the car, Helen asked, "Rebecca, do you know who the father of your child is?"

"Oh, yes", came her instant reply. "It couldn't be but one person. I mean, I've never been with but one person." Her face was red with embarrasement. "I've known him all my life. I really care for him."

"Does he know, Rebecca?"

"Oh, no. He's got no idea. I think he likes me but I haven't told him. I didn't want him to feel trapped. Besides, he was drunk and got locked up New Year's Eve. I haven't dated him since then although he has asked me out several times." Rebecca was not forth coming with a name, still trying to shield the boy.

"Well, first things first", Helen said. "When may we speak with your grandmother? Is she home now?"

"Y.e.s, Yes, Ma'am", Rebecca stammered.

"What about right now?" Helen suggested.

"I guess so", Rebecca replied. "Grandfather will not be home till 4 o'clock."

Surprised to see Rebecca home so early, and accompanied by Helen, Mrs. Ellis invited them into the living room to sit. With apprehension in her eyes, she said she remembered meeting Helen on Christmas Eve when the carolers came by. Helen, uncertain as to how to open the conversation began, "Mrs. Ellis, Rebecca has asked me to come with her. She has something to tell you."

Rebecca felt her face grow hot and a knot tighten up in her stomach. "Grandmother... Grandmother..."

"You're with child", Mrs. Ellis said.

"Yes, Grandmother", Rebecca said as she burst into tears.

"I'm sorry, Grandmother. I'm sorry I let you down."

"Oh, Precious Child, you didn't let me down. I've suspected it for a while. Why, you've always been our precious jewel and still are".

"How did you know?" Rebecca asked.

"Precious, I heard you throwing up early in the mornings when you thought I was asleep. I was wanting you to talk to me about it. Honey, who is the father?"

"Grandmother, I know who he is but I don't want to say right now."

Grandmother Ellis had no bitter words or recriminations, only love and concern for her only granddaughter. "We will help you through this", she said.

Giving Rebecca our phone number, Helen promised, "I'll be in touch." She then left them to be alone.

When Helen came home, she related everything to me. When she got to the part about the boy, the father, being drunk New Year's Eve and being locked up, that rang a bell with me. I mean to say, a red flag went up! The nagging recollection of being "behind bars" came rushing back. I pictured Ben and Bart and that red Ford. Besides the bad scenes though, I vividly remembered the Sunday morning the twins had made their way boldly to the altar to turn their lives around. As I recalled the time since then, I remembered seeing Ben speak to Rebecca as she paused momentarily and then hurried out the door, apparently not wanting to talk with him. I could be totally wrong but by deductive reasoning, I thought I had come to the right conclusion. I decided that Helen and I, working on two fronts, might intervene and help Rebecca with her delima.

The opportunity to see Ben came sooner than I expected. A couple of days later, he was getting gas at Harry Chance's store so I pulled in behind him.

"Hi, Pastor".

"Hi, Ben."

"Sure feels good being back in church", Ben said.

"I'm glad, Ben. Our food in Blue Ridge wasn't all that good."

"No, Sir, it wasn't", Ben said, recalling the jail.

"Say, Ben. There's a new girl at church named Rebecca Ellis. She's kinda shy and doesn't say much," I prodded.

"Yes, Sir. I know her. We grew up together. I mean, I'm three years older than she is but we were friends growing up. We dated a few times. But Pastor, why do you ask?"

I didn't answer specifically. "I understand that she was not feeling well this week. I thought you might know her.

"Yes Sir, she's a fine girl. I like her a lot but she doesn't seem to want to talk to me any more", Ben responded.

"Okay, thanks Ben."

I went into the store and spoke to Harry, giving Ben time to leave . After a brief conversation with Harry, I left for home.

After talking with Ben, I felt that he would check on Rebecca. I told Helen that she should plant the idea in Rebecca's mind to tell her child's father the truth. This, of course, was based on the assumption that we had correctly figured out this scenario.

CHAPTER 21

I didn't return to the peaceful seclusion of Silas and Dog for another three weeks. I prayed, "Oh, God, let the timing be right. This is not my vineyard, but Yours; I only tend it. And while I am digging, please don't let me harm the tender roots". So under the guise of an avid angler, I traipsed again up the valley. Most of the flowering trees had replaced blossoms with heavier green foliage. Only twenty-one days, but what a transformation in the flora in this majestic valley. The wide areas appeared to have become narrower with the coming of this canopy of green and now the floor was carpeted with violets, their delicate purple petals lifted up to God in a silent praise. The background of spring grass gave contrast, making them of particular notice. Here and there were shoots of wild onions and garlic, their pungent odor being pleasant to the eager nostril. I have often experienced spring days like this since I was a boy, but the wonder and accute awareness of supernatural splendor has never left me.

My marker was still in place. I took note of it and passed by until I came to the familiar clearing. My, how the green trees had closed in. I walked right up to the porch where Dog lazily stood up and stretched himself. He then offered me his paw to shake.

"Silas", I called. "You got a cool drink of water for a thirsty traveler?"

"You bet I do, by Ned," Silas responded. His voice was raspy but he seemed to be more "chipper" today.

"What you been up to?" I asked.

"I've been working on something."

"Good water, Silas, good spring water. What ya got?" I asked.

"I made it for you", he said as he handed me a beautiful hand-crafted knife with a deerskin scabbard. "You said you like knives. Made this one out of a crosscut saw blade".

I knew from boyhood what a crosscut saw was and I knew they were made of excellent steel. "Silas, I don't know what to say. I love it. It's one of the best presents I've ever been given." This brought tears to Silas' eyes.

"Preacher, excuse me, I mean Matthew. Is it okay with you for me to take off this old pile cap? This spring heat has got my head to itching."

"Sure, Silas, it's fine."

"Matthew, I've been thinking lots about that little Robin Jones wanting to meet Dog. You think maybe we could see her one evening at your house? We travel mostly in the evening. We wouldn't have to go in the house and bother your wife."

"Oh, Silas, you and Dog would be no bother to my wife. Her name is Helen and she would love having you. Tell ya what I'll do. Today is Wednesday. How 'bout Friday, five o'clock , you and Dog come to my house. I'll try to arrange for Robin to be there. But how will you know that I have everything worked out?" I questioned.

"If everything is arranged, you can hang that white canvas bag on your front porch. Dog and I need to go to town tomorrow evening anyway. If we see the bag, we'll know to come the next afternoon."

"Very good, Silas, very good."

I could barely believe my ears. Not only had he agreed to see Robin, but he actually seemed eager. Then the prayer about not injuring the tender roots became vivid in my mind and I knew that God had worked to help me cultivate this old, but tender, plant. I left Ole Silas that day with great excitement in my heart. I don't remember leaving the clearing or passing my marker. I guess I was on autopilot. I remember the violets, though. Their silent voices called out to me as I made my way through them, cautious not to crush any.

"Helen! Helen"! She dashed out of the house and came running toward me even though I was still fifty yards away.

"What is it, Darling?" she gasped.

Her face was flushed and I realized that my enthusiasm had startled her.

"Nothing bad, Honey." She took my arm as we walked to the porch.

"Honey, Ole Silas has agreed to let Robin meet Dog. If we can get Robin over here Friday evening, Silas will come by at 5 o'clock. I think he is coming out of his shell."

With Silas coming on Friday, Helen's wheels began turning. "Now let's see. We will need some refreshments. I'll bake a chocolate cake. I'll have coffee, oh yes, and lemonade available. Yes, and we will bring some more chairs out. How 'bout a tape player with some low music playing and a vase of fresh daffodils"? I knew she would handle all things well and enjoy immensely the labor therein.

"Helen, we have to talk to Alton and Sue after church tonight. If it's all right with them, I'd prefer that only Robin, you, and I be here with Silas. I think initially the less people present, the better. Oh yes, I must not forget to hang that canvas bag on the front porch tomorrow as a signal to Silas that everything has been arranged."

"Sounds a little intriguing with the secret signals and all", Helen responded.

"Yes, Honey, I guess that is a pretty good description of this whole episode. It continues to be very intriguing."

I asked Alton and Sue if they could stay for a few minutes after church to talk. I wanted to keep the meeting with Silas as much a secret as possible for the time being. When everyone was gone except their family, I explained the delicate nature of this meeting and asked if Robin could be there. They expressed surprise that Silas, who had secluded himself, or maybe I should say excluded himself, from the human race for all these years, should venture from his lair to make contact with anyone without necessity. Sue was understandably apprehensive about Robin meeting a mythical hermit, much less his dog. I related my experiences with Silas over the past few months, being careful not to be overheard by their children. After hearing about Silas, his life, and pain, Sue relented and they gave their permission for Robin to be there.

"Please keep this as secret as possible for now", I asked. They nodded in understanding agreement. I further assured them, "By the way, Dog wouldn't bite a biscuit!"

Alton asked the other three children to go to the car. Kneeling down in front of Robin's wheelchair, I asked, "My Little Yankee, can you keep a secret?"

"I think so", came her sincere reply.

"You remember about Ole Silas?"

"Yes, Sir".

"Well, you told me that you wanted to meet Dog and play with him."

"Yes, Sir".

"Would you like to come to our house Friday after school and meet Ole Silas and Dog?"

She hesitated a moment in serious thought. Then with dancing blue eyes, she gleefully asserted, "Yes! I'll wear my blue dress for him."

I knew the feminine decision was set once she started planning what she would wear; a familiar pattern I have observed in Helen during these ten years of marital bliss.

Everything being set and everyone sworn to secrecy, I proceeded to hang the canvas bag on the front porch in a prominent spot. Now the waiting began. All day Thursday, Helen was cheerfully going about the kitchen baking and planning like a woman on a mission, as I guess, she was. She loved to entertain and serve others but, as I was looking ahead, I thought this might be the strangest social event she had ever hosted. I prayfully contemplated this event with my ever present obsession in mind, that of winning Silas.

Sue was very prompt and had Robin at our house at 4:30.

"Robin has kept the secret well", Sue said. "The other children don't have a clue." She gave Robin last minute instructions, "Tell Mrs. Slater when you have to go to the bathroom."

It was now 4:45. Helen had the soft background music going, the cake was ready, the coffee hot, the lemonade cold. We had prepared Robin ahead of time for what she might expect to see and hear. Her long sandy hair and blue eyes told me that she would make a hit with Silas.

"Matthew, hello, Matthew", came that familiar raspy voice as

Silas came into view.

"Hey, Silas. Come up on the porch. This is my wife, Helen. Helen, I'd like you to meet my friend, Silas Vinson."

"Hello, Ma'am. I brought you these camellias. They were the last ones to bloom this year."

"Thank you, Mr. Vinson", Helen said. "I love flowers and these are beautiful. We are very happy to have you. This is our friend, Robin Jones. Robin, this is Mr. Silas".

"How do you do, Mr. Silas? Is that your dog?" Robin took over the conversation as Silas beamed at her childish enthusiasm. "I heard about Dog and I've wanted to meet him for a long time, ever since I was little."

Silas chuckled out loud. Little Robin quieted all fears and any reservations we may have had about this meeting. Timing, music, refreshments, all took a backseat to this little crippled girl.

"Let me tell you 'bout Dog", Silas began. I was coming back from Chance's store a few years ago. I almost stumbled over something in the dark. There on the side of the road, this little puppy was whimpering. I guess someone had put him out. He had mange real bad. His little stomach was swollen and he was so skinny that his ribs were showing. I carried him home with me and nursed him back to health. That's all the sound he would ever make, just a whimper. I found out later that he couldn't bark. He never has, not even at a rabbit."

"Will you have some coffee, Mr. Vinson, and some chocolate cake?" Helen offered.

"Yes, Ma'am".

Silas was dressed in fresh pressed overalls and a fresh shirt. His boots were clean, his beard neatly trimmed. I had mentally prepared Helen and Robin for his appearance so his cap received no particular attention.

"Real good cake, Ma'am, real good. My Molly used to bake a good chocolate cake, my favorite."

"Thank you. There's plenty more."

I could barely believe the ease with which conversation flowed. Dog lay passively still.

"Mr. Silas, do you think I could pet Dog?" Robin asked.

"Yes, Honey, I think Dog would like that. Dog, say hello to Robin".

Dog promptly stood up, went over to Robin's wheelchair, and offered his right paw. *Giggle! Giggle! Giggle*, Robin reacted as she took his paw. Dog licked her hand in mannerly approval and lay down beside her chair as she lovingly stroked his head and neck.

"Matthew, looks like Dog has really taken a liking to Robin. I can see why. She has eyes the color of our trout pond. They sparkle like it does when the sun shines on it."

"I'd say that was a pretty good description, Silas, pretty good."

"Mr. Silas, why do you wear that cap?" Robin asked.

Caught off guard, Silas stuttered, "I got burned real bad a long time ago."

Reaching over to Silas, Robin asked, "May I see?"

"Well, by Ned, why not?" at which time he slowly pulled his cap aside exposing the scars. Robin didn't react except to pet his cheek. The surprise at her acceptance of his gruesome appearance encouraged Silas to completely remove the cap. I saw Helen swallow hard a couple of times and wipe her eyes when Silas wasn't looking.

"Why don't you come to church with us sometime?" Robin blurted out. She cut right through the rhetoric and diplomacy I would have used, and arrived instantly at the precise point I would have arrived. She only accomplished it weeks earlier than I would have.

"Well, why don't you just get out of that rolling chair and walk?" Silas retorted.

He didn't say it sarcastically or ugly or out of anger. He just said it matter-of-factly.

"Well, maybe I will", she exclaimed with an amused look on her face. She wasn't hurt; she was challenged.

"I'll go to church with you the next Sunday after you walk", Silas agreed.

She took a deep breath and responded, "You got a deal, Mr. Silas. Shake on it!"

Ole Silas was amazed at her spirit and amused by her intellect. As he felt Robin's tiny hand grasping for his, a dam burst inside his soul and a flood of hideous pain was soothed with this balm of newfound warmth and acceptance.

"By, Ned, this girl's got spunk!"

"I almost forgot", Helen said, as she went into the house. She returned with a big bone for Dog. "I was cooking some greens and used this ham bone for seasoning. Is it okay to give it to Dog?"

"Yes, Ma'am, and thank you. Dog shake hands with Mrs. Slater."

As the sun dropped behind the hills, Silas remarked, "I'd better be going toward home."

"Can you come back next Friday to give me walking lessons, you and Dog?" asked Robin.

"Well", he stuttered, "well"...

"Can you Silas?" I asked.

"Well, yes, if you think it would be all right."

So we, all four, five counting Dog, agreed to have walking lessons on Friday next. Sue and Alton were elated at the idea that Robin was challenged to walk. Sue confided, "The Doctors said that she has nerve damage and they didn't give us much hope that she will walk again. We welcome encouragement for her." As we reflected on the evening's events and before peaceful sleep overtook me, I whispered, "She must walk before he can crawl!"

CHAPTER 22

On Saturday, Helen took Rebecca shopping and bought her a lovely dress and matching shoes. Next stop was the beauty salon. When all was done, Rebecca looked very pretty.

Just before time for church to start Sunday morning, Ben hurried in and took a seat beside Rebecca. I observed when I could, but I didn't want them to see me see them. Helen's observations and mine, however, overlapped so we had a pretty good idea what was going on. Ben whispered something and took Rebecca's hand. She pulled away at first, but then reached for his hand. "It appears we were exactly right after all", I thought.

After church, Rebecca invited Ben to her house for lunch. She acted as if everything were normal. Her grandfather didn't know anything about her situation and Grandmother Ellis didn't say anything. Ben could feel her eyes on him although she was very hospitable. After lunch, Rebecca helped Mrs. Ellis in the kitchen while Mr. Ellis entertained Ben in the living room.

"...Handsome young man, Rebecca".

"Yes, Ma'am, he is, isn't he?"

Mrs. Ellis knew by Rebecca's expression and tone of voice that Ben was the father of her child. "Grandmother, I know he cares for me but I don't want to force him".

Mrs. Ellis took Rebecca in her arms. "I understand, Precious, I really do understand. Okay, you and that young man go on. It's a bright sunny day. Yall go for a ride and enjoy the afternoon."

Anxious to be out from under Mrs. Ellis' scrutiny, Ben didn't tarry, but politely said goodbye and walked Rebecca directly to the car. "You have very fine grandparents, Rebecca."

"Yes, they have been wonderful to me since Mom and Dad were killed in the car crash. Ben, may we go to the church yard and talk?"

"Sure, but don't you think that is a strange place to go and talk?"

"Some things are best said at church", she replied.

Ben felt the seriousness of the request but was completely puzzled as to the reason. Was she going to tell him that she was terminally ill with cancer or something like that?! Arriving at church, Ben stopped the car and rolled down the windows. The radio was playing softly and a gentle breeze was blowing.

Rebecca searched for words, but finding none, was preceeded by Ben as he said, "I wanted to talk with you the other day but you were in a hurry to leave. I've asked you out several times lately but you've always had something else to do. I thought you liked me, Rebecca."

"I do like you, Ben. I like you a lot. I've had a crush on you since I was nine years old, you knew that."

"No, I didn't know that", he said smiling.

"I was nine and you were twelve", she responded.

"I guess I was too dumb to see it, Rebecca. You've always been the sweetest girl around here." Ben continued, "I saw Pastor Slater at Chance's store the other day. He mentioned that you have not been feeling well. I was really concerned until I saw you looking so pretty in church this morning. You look great!"

"Ben, how much do you care for me?"

This direct question hit Ben broadside. He thought for a moment but didn't know how to respond. Eventually he answered. "I care for you a lot, Rebecca. I have for a long time. I don't know what to call it. I know I want to be with you."

The sun was shining through the windshield and the car had become really warm. With the heat and the state of her nerves right now, Rebecca felt nauseated. "I feel sick", she said, and opened the door and threw up. Ben helped her as best he could.

"Baby, I'm sorry you feel bad. Do you want to go home?" Ben helped her stand up. He held her head against his shoulder until she felt better. "Baby, what can I do?" Ben asked.

"Hold me, Ben. Just hold me".

After Rebecca was feeling better, they sat in the car again. "Have you been feeling badly very long?" Ben asked. "I don't understand. You were fine this morning and at lunch".

"I mostly don't feel good in the mornings and when it's too hot."

Ben's face grew pale and he became quiet. He looked at Rebecca with a bewildered expression. "You're pregnant!"

"Yes, I am", she sobbed.

A big grin came on Ben's face. Rebecca instinctively slapped him really hard.

"Don't make fun of me, it's your child", she cried.

"Oh, Rebecca, Baby, I'm not making fun of you. I'm happy. I love babies and I love you. I want to be with you. I want to marry you".

"Ben, I love you, too, but I don't want you to marry me out of obligation. You are free from that responsibility. You can walk away right now and nothing will ever be said. No one will ever know."

Her voice had such a believable note of sincerity and finality that Ben was grieved. He assured her in loving whispers that he wanted her and their baby. "When is he due?" Ben asked.

"He?!" she exclaimed.

"Okay, okay. *IT*... When is it due?"

"Doctor McPherson said five and a half months, just five and a half months".

Ben took Rebecca home that night after church to talk with her grandparents. He told them of their plans to marry as soon as possible. The next day Ben came by the church office on his lunch hour to tell me their plans. He asked me if I would perform the ceremony. I told him that I wanted to have a counseling session with them before I committed myself. He agreed to bring Rebecca by the church office the next evening at 5:30.

As they arrived, both were very nervous. "Please be seated and be at ease. I want to have prayer before we start," I said. After praying for wisdom and guidance, I began: "Rebecca, Ben tells me that the two of you want to be married".

"Yes sir ".

"Why?"

"We love each other," Ben interrupted.

"Yes, I know, Ben, but love is a word we toss around and use when it sounds good. Sometimes we use it because it sounds sexy or romantic or whatever we want it to sound like, depending on our state of mind. What I want to know, Rebecca, is do you want to marry this man because you are pregnant with his child and feel trapped, or do you love him and want to be his wife whether or not a child is involved?"

"Pastor, I wanted to marry Ben long before I became pregnant", Rebecca cried.

"Now, Ben, did you love Rebecca before she became pregnant or do you now feel love for her out of pity? Do you want to marry her because you feel trapped?"

"Pastor, I've always had feelings for Rebecca. I didn't call it love before. No sir, I don't feel trapped at all. When she told me about her, our, pregnancy, I was proud to be the father. I know we have done wrong but both of us have asked God's forgiveness. Yes, I do love her very much. Even if she wouldn't marry me, I would still love and support our child".

I watched Rebecca's admiration for Ben as he took responsibility and boldly stated his love and commitment to her. In both their eyes, I saw what I was looking for, that genuine caring for each other.

"Getting married is a natural thing. Having babies is a natural thing. Yall just got them in the wrong order. I will be honored to perform the wedding ceremony and Helen and I will help you in any way we can."

They both hugged me. "Thank you, Pastor" Ben said. "I'll do my best to be a good husband and father".

"I know you will, Ben".

Rebecca asked Helen to help her plan the wedding. Something about weddings just fascinates women. Helen was hereby fascinated. She talked with Rebecca and her grandmother to find out their wishes. They wanted a small, private mid-week wedding as soon as possible since the biological clock was ticking. Rebecca asked Helen to be her attendant with Bart as bestman. Only family would be present which would include Mr. and Mrs. Ellis and Millie Anderson. Mrs. Chastain would play the organ and, besides her, there would be no others except me. I knew that since this is a small community, news travels fast. For the sake of all involved, I was glad to put this behind us with as little publicity as possible. I felt confident that Rebecca and Ben, who had started out so badly, would certainly live happily ever after.

CHAPTER 23

Today was my day off. April was radiant, as Aprils are; apple blossoms, plum and pear trees boasting fragrant flowers in competition with the white blossoms of the Dogwood. And yes, my favorite was well represented in these hills, the wild crab apple with its delicate pink flower.

This new life had been well watered so far this spring. The day became overcast early and by noon, it was almost dark. The wind, which had been blowing all morning as the clouds moved in, ceased noticeably. All was still and a quiet, eerie calm prevailed. The thick, low, looming clouds over-shadowed us with apprehension. And then, **too late**, the warning...**TORNADO**... flashed over the radio.

Roaring over the hills, it swept up the valley cutting a swath of devastation as it skipped along settling down where it would, like a child playing hopscotch. Here a roof, there a barn; trees lying down in humble obeyance to its bidding. People call it an act of God. I beg to differ. The devil comes to steal, kill, and destroy. John 10:10. This fits his job description perfectly. I turned my radio to the emergency station and found that power had been knocked out to the whole area and that many trees had been blown down across all the roads leading out of Stone Gap. We had effectively been encapsulated in our community with no outside help available. My mind raced, thinking of the possible injuries there might be. With no emergency personnel or local law enforcement in Stone Gap, I knew the church must respond quickly to the need. Miraculously, the telephone was still working.

"Hello, Mrs. Chastain, are you all right? Thank God! Is the church damaged?"

She said the church was not damaged except for some limbs which were blown down. I called Dr. McPherson at the clinic. He said he had an emergency generator and that he and Paula could handle any critical injuries until transfer could be made to Blue Ridge. We agreed to have less critical cases come to the church where Helen could begin first aid. Mrs. Chastain would operate as a switchboard command center at the church with the regular church line for the public and my private number for communication with the clinic.

"Mrs. Chastain, please call and see who can supply camp stoves, blankets, lanterns, flashlights, water, emergency medical kits, food, coffee, and anything else you can think of. Call the Anderson boys and ask them to be runners. Please hurry while the phones are still working."

Mrs. Chastain is a real workhorse and I knew my instructions were in capable hands. The hail and black-blinding rain that ensued made it almost impossible to see the road as Helen and I drove to the church. The intermittent bold flashes of lightning only further blinded us and hampered our progress.

Within an hour, Tommy arrived with the first installment of three cots and some blankets. John Mason came in from the mill and said his back porch had sustained some damage but the rest of the house was okay. "Thank God, our Lord, Sarah wasn't hurt. Tommy, is Paula okay at the clinic?" John asked.

"Yes sir, she's fine but very busy. I'm going over there when I leave here."

"I'm glad. I know she's in good hands when she's with you, Son."

They shook hands and smiled.

"Tommy will you stop and pick up Mrs. Odessa Smith? She needs to go to the clinic."

John said, "Pastor, my men and I have brought our jeeps and saws so we'll be clearing some of the trees off the roads."

"That's good thinking, John. Please see that the way is clear between the church and the clinic first. You can coordinate with Mrs. Chastain."

"I'm thankful for our food bank here at church", I thought. "Today may bring home the true meaning of benevolence".

Ben and Bart appeared shortly after Tommy. "Pastor, what can we do?"

"Men, there are lots of injured people who need to be transported from the clinic to the church, or from the church to the clinic, or from the village to either place. This is a big emergency and we won't have any outside help until tomorrow at the earliest. Can you make ambulance runs? "

"Yes, sir," they said with one voice.

Before I knew what was happening, they had removed the passenger seat of their car and installed a cot in its place and used another cot for a litter. "Wonderful, men, that's wonderful," I commended.

As the calls came in, Mrs. Chastain would dispatch the boys in the red Ford ambulance on their errands of mercy. Harry Chance brought plastic sheeting to give to any who needed a roof patch or weatherproofing for broken windows. Millie Anderson arrived and immediately took a position as Helen's assistant. Harry and I rearranged the pews to form rows of beds.

"Mrs. Chastain, if you can find time, please go down the church roll and call each family. Log any injuries, needs, or property damage."

The injured and those without shelter began steadily staggering into the sanctuary. Many were in a state of shock. Some had superficial bruises and abrasions. One lady obviously had a broken leg, and two more had broken arms. We immediately calmed them down and called for Ben and Bart to transfer them to the clinic.

"Oh, yes, Guys, on the return trip, please have Dr. McPherson send us lots of bandages if he can spare them."

"Pa, Ma Mac, what are you doing here? Are you and Sammy and Alicia all right?"

"Yes, Pastor, we're just fine. We came to help with the injured."

Just as if they had been trained to help in medical emergencies, they went about their chores of heating soup and coffee, pacifying children, changing diapers, and whatever their hands found to do.

At the clinic, Tommy found Dr. McPherson and Paula overloaded with patients having serious injuries. Many broken bones had to be set, many lacerations had to be sewn up. Tommy helped Dr. McPherson set the broken bones which freed Paula to administer stitches to those who needed them and give tetanus shots to many more. Tommy by now had an apron which, like the others, was blood spattered. "You're doing quite well, Tommy", said Dr. McPherson.

"I saw a lot of this in Vietnam", Tommy replied. His first hand experience and steady nerves made him a valuable asset.

Paula smiled, "You're a good man to have around".

The rain subsided around 10:00 p.m. An eerie blackness hung over the village, a black calm; no lights except lanterns and flashlights.

"By Ned, it's dark as Egypt out there."

It was Ole Silas. I didn't call his name for reasons of anonymity. I just said, "Come in, Old Friend". Are you all right?"

"Right as rain" he said. "Matthew, I would have been here sooner but I can't see very well at night and the rain was really blinding."

"Is your place okay?" I asked.

"By Ned, it's strong as a fort. How 'bout little Robin? Is she okay?"

"Yes, I think so. Let's check with Mrs. Chastain. Mrs. Chastain, this is Mr. Vinson. Do you have any word on Alton Jones and his family?"

"Yes, Pastor, they are all okay."

"Is little Robin okay?" Silas insisted.

"Yes, Mr. Vinson, they were all in the dark but said the children were enjoying playing by candlelight."

"That's just fine," Silas sighed. "Been worried 'bout her since the storm hit."

Silas was not very sociable with many people, though he did talk to Helen, me, and occasionally, Mrs. Chastain. He certainly was helpful moving things around, gathering up garbage, and generally just being there. Everyone and everything was so disshelved that nobody seemed to notice Silas' pile cap. The first rays of a new day forced their way over the mountain peaks and eventually pierced the mist as they sifted down to flowers and trees that were awaiting illumination. A glorious new day, clear and fresh, had arrived which would show us the devastation of yesterday. I knew there was extensive damage by the number of injured, both at church and at the clinic. I heard the distant sound of chain saws all night and into the early morning hours and I knew that many trees had fallen.

Dr. McPherson looked at Paula and Tommy and said, "You two are going to make a fine couple. You really work well together." Tommy had consoled many of the patients receiving stitches as Paula expanded her "on the job training".

By 10 o'clock a.m. the roads were clear enough for ambulances to come from Blue Ridge for the most seriously injured. By noon the clinic looked almost normal except for an excess amount of red mud on the floor.

"Tommy, take Paula home. Paula, get some rest and please call me around 6 o'clock; I may need you this evening."

"Silas", I blurted out without thinking, "thank you very much". He grasped my hand firmly, then turned and walked away without a word.

"Is that Ole Silas?" Mrs. Chastain stammered. I nodded. "He's really very nice", she said.

With all the people gone now from church, we went home to get some much -needed rest.

The people of the village and the surrounding farms went back to their daily lives and eventually repaired and rebuilt houses and barns. Thank God, that with all the injuries, there was no loss of life. There was, however, a large supply of firewood sawed from fallen trees, compliments of the storm.

CHAPTER 24

Friday evening came around again and "walking school" was convened on our front porch. "Come on, little Robin." Silas would coach her as Helen or I would take her hand. We spent hours with her on her feet. Although she hadn't taken a step, I knew her legs had to be getting stronger.

The days were warm now so we started having our sessions on the front lawn. Robin, or "Little Bird" as Silas called her now, really worked hard and began to take short, laborious steps, but still dragged her left foot. After each session Helen would give her a therapeutic leg message. Results were very slow in coming but we all felt that we were making progress. Then, one Friday evening after about an hour of practice, Robin sat back in her chair to watch Dog cross the road. Just as he was coming out of the pasture across the road from our yard, he ran in front of a car. The car was going very slowly and fortunately only bumped Dog. The blow, however, was enough to spin him around. and then something really strange happened. Dog barked at the car as it went on down the road, the driver totally oblivious to the whole event.

"Dog," Silas summoned as Dog obeyed. All eyes were on Dog but, as we were watching him, Robin stood to her feet and started walking toward Dog, crying as she went.

"Dog, Dog, please don't die". Unaware of her mobility, she threw her arms around his neck as he affectionately wagged his tail. For an unbelievable moment, not a word was spoken. Then the silence was broken.

"Thank God, by Ned, she walked".

Silas repeated this again as he danced around. Helen and I joined him dancing and frolicking in a joyous demonstration. When we were worn out, and out of breath, we all dried our eyes and sat down to see what Robin would do. At first, she didn't realize what she had done. But then her little mind began to grasp the idea that she had, in fact, walked. She very slowly began to walk to Silas.

"I thought Dog, my friend, might die."

"No, Little Bird, Dog has lived to help you walk".

"I didn't think I could walk. I was afraid to try. When Dog got hurt, I had to go to him", she whimpered.

"Everything's gonna be all right now," Silas whispered, his eyes full of tears, "Ole Silas has gotta get a haircut, Little Bird... got church Sunday".

Robin smiled. We laughed, we cried, we laughed and cried some more. Robin walked back over to Dog, took him by the collar, and began walking slowly around the yard.

Sue and Alton couldn't believe their eyes as they drove up and saw Robin walking..

"Praise the Lord, Praise the Lord, Thank you Jesus" rang out as they hugged Robin and then each other.

We all collaborated with Robin's parents to surprise everyone Sunday morning. We agreed that Robin should remain in her wheelchair until Silas could walk in with her. It was all we could do to restrain ourselves from sharing our good news that evening.

"Matthew, you have already done so much for me, I hate to ask. I haven't been to a barbershop in years. Would you, well, I mean, if you don't mind, could you go with me to the barbershop?"

"Silas, it would be my pleasure. When do you want to go? "

"Right now", Silas replied. "Is it still open?"

"Let's see...6:30: I think so. Let me call Ned and find out".

"Sure, Pastor, I stay open late on Friday anyway." I prepared Ned for Silas' appearance.

Silas confided that he didn't want to wait until the next morning because so many people would be there. "This late, maybe nobody will see me", he said.

"Hi, Ned."

"Hi, Pastor".

While introducing these two big men, I felt small with my 5'9" stature. We were in luck. Because of the lateness of the hour, no one else was there. Silas got into the chair and slowly removed his cap.

"Bad scar", Ned said very forthrightly.

"By Ned, you're right there, Son, and no use trying to deny it".

"Is it tender anywhere, Mr. Vinson?"

"No, not at all."

"How do you want it?"

"Make me look good for Sunday church. Also, please trim my beard."

"Okay," Ned replied, "I'll give you my Sunday special."

Ole Silas was transformed.

"Ned, add a bottle of that cologne to my bill", he said.

Silas paid him and we both thanked him again.

"See you in church, Pastor. Nice to meet you, Mr. Vinson."

"Silas, you're welcome to ride to church with Helen and me."

"Yes, Matthew, I'd be much obliged. What time do you leave home?"

"Nine o'clock will be fine", I said.

As I would have expected, Silas was right on time. He had on a well pressed suit and tie that was obviously out-dated. His shoes, though worn, were shined to prefection. He did not wear his cap, only carried it in his hand. What a giant step he must be taking by unveiling himself and taking a leap from darkness into the light.

Since this was Memorial Day weekend, I planned to recognize our veterans and to let those speak who wanted to. Mrs. Chastain was already there when we arrived. I asked her to let Silas use her office until we were ready for him to escort Robin into the sanctuary. I had arranged with Alton to save the two aisle seats on his row for them. Now we just waited for the church to fill up. Tommy and Paula kept Robin outside awaiting my signal.

As the congregation sang *"Only Believe, all things are possible, only believe"* , I could hardly contain my joy. When everyone was seated and waiting for me to speak, I began: *"Only believe, only believe. All things are possible, only believe.* Miracles have not ceased for those who believe. Today we witness such a miracle".

As I looked toward the back of the sanctuary, Tommy and Paula opened the doors. Silas and Robin slowly entered as the congregation responded in silent amazement. Tears, smiles, praises, laughter, and then a thunderous round of applause went up. I don't think very many people even knew who Silas was. Mrs. Chastain played *"Because He Lives"* as we sang in thanks and worship to God. Everyone truly had reason to praise Him this morning.

"I don't have a sermon today. It has already been given. I shall attempt to comment on it, however. The Lord is good."

Again, a thunderous applause broke out.

"We see and know that God is good. Though we may not always understand it, we still know it. We see before us a child whom the Doctors said would probably never walk again, but God said she would. The tornado's blackness and fury seemed to say that the sun wouldn't shine again, but it did. The first splintery rays of the majestic sun whispered at dawn 'oh, boisterous and foolish storm, be gone, for God has ordained a new day.' Yes, God is good, for we live as millions before have only dreamed of living, and in a place, nothing less than a paradise to those who dreamed those dreams; And it is ours. Yes, God is good."

I continued, "We are honored to have with us some of the people who have helped secure that dream, some of the veterans of our military services. Today we would like to honor these men and offer our heartfelt thanks to them. As I call your name, please stand. After every name has been called, each may speak if he desires.

Ned Benson	Navy, Mediterranean
Harry Chance	Marine Corp, Korea
John Ellis	Army, France
Alton Jones	Army, Germany
Tommy Jones	Army, Vietnam
Charles Kiser	Navy, Pacific
Matthew Slater	Army, Germany
James Turner	Army, Korea
Silas Vinson	Army, Belgium

Each man stood proudly and spoke briefly. The common thread of freedom, pride of service, and love of country seemed to weave its way through each testimony. I concluded the service with "God is good. Amen".

As Helen, Silas, and I drove slowly toward our house, Helen said, "Mr. Vinson, we were so very pleased that you came this morning. Please promise that you will come back again."

Helen said it with so much conviction that Silas responded, "Oh, Yes Ma'am, I will or my name is not Silas Johnston Vinson."

"Silas", I exclaimed. "Say that again, your name."

"Silas Johnston Vinson".

"Good name", I said. My mind was whirling, spinning out of control, as lights began coming on in my head.

"Mr. Vinson, will you come in for lunch?" Helen invited.

"No, Ma'am but thank you. I've had quite an exciting morning. I'm gonna lie down and rest this afternoon."

After Silas left for home, I told Helen that I was going in the study for a while.

"Are you all right? Don't you feel well?" she asked.

"Oh, yes, Honey, I'm fine. I just need to make some notes."

My mind was going faster than my pen as I scribbled some ideas.

" Hello, Ned, this is Matthew Slater".

"Hello, Pastor".

"I'm sorry to bother you but I'm doing some research. I need you to help me with it. I know this is going to be a weird request, but can you come to my house right away?"

"Sure, Pastor, I'll be right over."

"And, Ned, ...please wear some hiking shoes."

We had cancelled evening services because of the holiday weekend. "Helen", I said with some urgency, "I need a sandwich quickly. I have to go to Silas' cabin."

I gobbled my sandwich down in eager anticipation of the coming afternoon. When Ned arrived, he had a quizzical expression on his face. "Pastor, this is a lovely day for a hike", he said playfully.

"Ned, I know you are fond of hiking and, with such a lovely afternoon, I 'd like you to go with me to see Ole Silas. There is some beautiful scenery along the way.

"Pastor, didn't he like his haircut"? Ned joked.

"Nothing like that", I laughed.

I guess I just about wore Ned out walking so fast. I panted with excitement as we broke into the clearing near Silas' house. Dog spotted us and wagged his tail as we approached.

"Silas, Ole Friend, this is Matthew", I called out.

"By, Ned", he said as he came out on the porch.

Surprised to see Ned and me, he finally said, "Come, sit on the porch".

After talking for a few minutes, I asked Silas if I could show Ned inside his cabin. As he looked around, Ned stopped dead still, staring at the picture on the wall. After what seemed like several minutes, he pulled a picture from his wallet. His eyes filled with tears. "It's the same picture", he mumbled. Groping for words... "the same eyes, the same hair, the same dress... Where did it come from?"

We went back to where Silas was sitting on the porch. "Silas, Ned asked about the picture of Penny," I said. "Please tell us the story about her".

Silas recounted the history of his relationship with Penny.

"Was she from Vinings, Silas?" Ned asked.

"Why, yes she was, Ned. Why do you ask, Son?"

Handing Silas the picture from his wallet, Ned said, "My mother was from Vinings. Her name was Penelope Pope."

Silas gasped! "I haven't heard that name in over forty years. I don't understand."

As I took my notes from my pocket, I began. "Silas, you went overseas, July 1, 1942. Isn't that right?"

"Yes."

"You received letters from Penny until April, 1943, when she died, isn't that right?"

"Yes".

"Ned was born March 30, 1943. Isn't that right, Ned?"

"Yes."

"Ned told me months ago that his middle name was *Johnston* after his father's middle name. Many southern boys are named Lee after Robert E. Lee, or Jackson after Stonewall Jackson, but I have never heard of anyone else but you two who were named after Johnston. Ned said he didn't know where his mother got his first name but I think I do!"

"By, Ned", Silas beamed, "I think I do, too!! Penny used to tease me about saying 'By Ned' so much."

"I can't believe it, Pastor," Ned said. "This is unreal."

"I think what happened", I responded, "is that there was bad communication about the last name on the birth certificate... *Benson... Vinson...* Apparently Penny wanted her son to have your name, Silas, but it wasn't written down correctly before she died. If this were not the way it happened, Ned's last name would have been Pope."

"Oh, Mr. Vinson!...Silas...Tell me about my mom. I never knew her. I was only six days old when she died. I only know what was written on the birth certificate Mother left for me when she realized she was dying."

"Son, that third headstone over there is for Penny. Although she is not buried there, I still wanted to have a place for her."

"Silas, Ned, I'll leave you two alone for a while. Dog would probably like to take a walk with me."

They sat there in unbelief, unraveling the tangled threads of their past and fusing memories into a common framework of intelligible understanding.

I don't know all that went on or all that was discussed that Sunday afternoon on Memorial Day weekend, but I do know that Father and Son met and filled a place in each other's life; a place that had been empty for many, many years. Ole Silas would never again be the recluse he had been. His enlightenment included a daughter-in-law, two grandsons, and a granddaughter.

CHAPTER 25

A wedding was in the air. The buzz of corner conversion at church was about flowers, dresses, and bridesmaids. Paula wanted Katie to be her maid-of-honor. She would be home from school by then. Bridesmaids would be Sue Jones, Helen, and Shirley Farley. Tommy wanted Alton to be his best man. The ushers would be Ben and Bart Anderson. To this entourage was added an adorable little girl some called Robin, others "Little Yankee", and still others "Little Bird"; but this day they would call her "Flower Girl".

Tommy had worked feverishly the past three months building the house where he would take Paula as his bride. It would have been already finished had the tornado not hampered its progress. With the wedding only two weeks away, it was going to be a tight schedule but he believed he could complete it on time. John Mason had really taken a liking to Tommy and helped him with clearing and landscaping. Others volunteered for various jobs painting, and cleaning up. Tommy worked every day from very early to very late. Paula went over after she left the clinic and took him supper and worked with him all evening. Like Dr. McPherson had observed, "they really worked well together". Paula's prayer, symbolized by her Christmas tree ornament of praying hands, had been answered in intricate detail.

The Anderson boys are driving slower these days and have even taken off the glass packs. On a warm June evening, if one is really aware, he might see a red Ford quietly cruising around the nearest ice cream parlor with Bart driving, and a brown haired beauty named Katie sitting beside him.

Aaron and Daisy McHenry seem to have more vitality now that they have Sammy and Alicia living with them. It still amazes me to see a man that old playing softball.

Ned and his family have opened their arms wide to Grandpa Silas, the fulfillment of a lifelong dream for both Ned and Silas.

Little Robin is walking, running, playing, and pushing Dog around in her wheelchair. There is talk of a pink bicycle.

Maybe it's nesting time, who knows? Silas is getting to church pretty early these days. Mrs. Chastain finds many chores for him. This requires long and frequent discussions in her office. He seems to take to this like a duck to water.

And so turns the earth. If we only take time to observe, some quiet evening or some lazy summer day, we may be wise enough to recognize heaven come down and to see God's glory, which He shares in His time and in His place. To such a place I have come. This is my call, Call to the Blue Ridge, a vibrant, never ending call to live, to worship, to serve.

* * * * *

If you have a need in your life or if you, like Tommy, are thirsty, Jesus Christ is inviting you to the water where He will satisfy the thirstiest soul. *"But whosoever drinketh of the water that I shall give him shall never thirst". St. John 4:14a*